Better
Off
Wed

**Center Point
Large Print**

**This Large Print Book carries the
Seal of Approval of N.A.V.H.**

Better Off Wed

LAURA DURHAM

CENTER POINT PUBLISHING
THORNDIKE, MAINE

This Center Point Large Print edition
is published in the year 2005 by arrangement with
Avon Books, an Imprint of HarperCollins Publishers.

The text of this Large Print edition is unabridged. In other
aspects, this book may vary from the original edition. Printed in
Thailand. Set in 16-point Times New Roman type.

ISBN 1-58547-645-5

Library of Congress Cataloging-in-Publication Data

Durham, Laura.
    Better off wed / Laura Durham.--Center Point large print ed.
        p. cm.
    ISBN 1-58547-645-5 (lib. bdg. : alk. paper)
    1. Large type books. I. Title.

PS3604.U735B48 2005
813'.6--dc22

                                                            2005006443

For my parents,
who filled our home with an endless supply of love
and books.

Acknowledgments

Heartfelt thanks to my mentor and friend, Noreen Wald, whose considerable skills helped shape a single paragraph idea into a book series. To the Saturday morning writing group—Barb, Tim, Mary, John, Jack, and Carolyn—thank you for your insight and ideas. I am grateful to the Rector Lane Irregulars—Carla, Donna, Ellen, Noreen, Peggy, Sandi, and Val—for their invaluable critique. My sincere appreciation to my agent, Peter Rubie, and my editor, Sarah Durand, for taking a chance on a new author.

To my fabulous friends in the wedding industry— Ric, Jenny, Monte, Lisa, Anne, Diana, Andrea, Mary, Nancy, Karen, Michelle, Nick, the Catherines, The Mafia Girls, and so many more—who have been a source of inspiration and have helped me stay sane over the years. Thank you to the hundreds of brides, both the delightful and the deranged, whose weddings have given me stories for countless books.

My deepest thanks to Mom, Dad, James, Liz, Lua, and all my dear friends and family, for continuing to provide unwavering support. Finally, much love to Juan Carlos for filling my days with joy.

Chapter 1

Planning a wedding can be murder. Planning weddings for a living is nothing short of suicide.

"Is there a patron saint for wedding consultants? Because I think after this wedding, I just might meet the requirements." I stood near the top of the wide marble staircase that swept down the middle of the Corcoran Gallery of Art's central foyer. Below me, dozens of tuxedo-clad waiters scurried around the enormous hall filled end to end with tables and gold ladder-backed chairs. After having draped ivory chiffon into swags on all forty tables, I massaged the red indentations left on my fingers by the heavy pins.

"Annabelle, darling, I may be a lapsed Catholic, but I'm pretty sure you have to be dead to qualify for sainthood." Richard Gerard has been one of my closest friends since I arrived in Washington, D.C. three years ago and started "Wedding Belles." At the time, he'd been the only top caterer who'd bother talking to a new wedding planner. Now I worked with him almost exclusively.

"The wedding isn't over yet."

"At least your suffering hasn't been in vain." Richard motioned at the room below us. "It's divine."

The museum's enormous hall did look magical. The side railings of the staircase were draped with a floral garland, leading to a pair of enormous white rose topiaries flanking the bottom of the stairs. Amber light washed each of the three-story limestone columns bordering the room, and white organza hung from the ceiling, creating sheer curtains that were tied back at each column with clusters of ivory roses.

"I just hope the MOB is happy." My smile disappeared as I thought of the Mother of the Bride, Mrs. Clara Pierce. I started down the stairs to double-check the tables.

"I don't think she does 'happy.'" Richard followed, his long legs catching up to me quickly.

"If I'd known she would make my life so miserable, I wouldn't have taken this wedding." I brushed a long, auburn strand of hair out of my face and tucked it back into my tight bun. I wore my hair up to make me look older and more experienced, but it didn't make me feel any different. I still got butterflies in my stomach at every wedding I planned.

"You must be kidding, darling." Richard lowered his voice as we reached the floor and a waiter walked past us. "This event is your ticket to all the big, society weddings."

"If society weddings mean more women like Mrs. Pierce, then I'm not interested." I leaned over the table closest to me and smoothed one of the organza bow napkin ties.

"Well, sure, she's been difficult . . ." Richard came behind me and fluffed the bow back up.

"Difficult?" I narrowed my eyes at Richard and picked up another napkin. "I had to drive her fifteen-year-old, incontinent poodle to the church this after-noon."

"Her dog was a guest?"

"Not a guest. The ring bearer." I watched as Richard began to shake with laughter. "Turns out there wasn't enough room in the limousine for the wedding party and Muffles, so I got the honors."

"Look at the bright side." Richard ran a hand through his dark, choppy hair. "You're barely thirty, and you beat out all those older consultants for this wedding."

"Probably because I charge less than they do. The first thing I'm doing on Monday is raising my rates." I picked up an unlit votive candle, and Richard produced a long, butane lighter from his suit pocket.

"Then we're going shopping." Richard gave me the once-over and shook the flame of the lighter at me. "If I see you in one more pantsuit, I'm going to cry."

"But they're so practical for working." I looked down at my "lucky" navy blue suit. "Lucky" because the long jacket covered up the fact that I'd been eating way too much take-out. "And this one is silk."

"It's a blend." Richard shook his head as he rubbed the fabric of my jacket lapel between his fingers. "If you want to be an A-list wedding planner, then we're going to have to dress you like one."

"Fine. As long as you promise not to go overboard."

"When would I ever go overboard?" The spread collar of Richard's fuchsia and green Versace shirt peeked out from underneath his black four-button suit.

My eyes darted to his neck, and I cleared my throat.

11

"You don't like the shirt?" Richard extended his arm so I could see the French cuffs. "It looks just darling with my white linen suit. I'd have worn that tonight but I never wear white before Memorial Day."

"Thank God for small favors."

"Speaking of doing favors, I'm also going to take you to the makeup counter. What's the use of having great cheekbones if you don't accentuate them?"

"I appreciate the flattery, Richard, but I don't like to wear lots of makeup."

"No kidding." Richard studied my face. "I'm amazed you look half decent with that drugstore garbage. Imagine how great you'd look if you used a designer line."

"I'll think about it."

"It would be cruel to tease me." Richard formed his lips into a pout.

"If there's any teasing to be done, I should be the one to do it." My assistant, Kate, came down the staircase behind us, her high heels clicking on each step. Kate always wore heels to weddings to show off her legs and make her look taller. She said you never knew who you might see at a wedding, and I was pretty sure she didn't mean old family friends.

"How's it going upstairs?" Richard asked. The nearly four hundred guests were being served cocktails on the upper level of the museum, which overlooked the foyer.

"Well, the sushi chefs almost quit because Mrs. Pierce timed them and took notes on their presentation."

"That damn notebook again." I rubbed my temples with my index fingers. "I can't believe she actually brought it to her daughter's wedding."

"Have you ever heard of someone making notes each time you do something she doesn't like?" Kate put a hand on my arm for support as she stepped out of her heels.

"There are a lot of things I'd never heard of before I became a wedding planner," I said. "After working for Mrs. Pierce, I've seen it all."

"Tell me about it." Kate flicked her short blond hair off her face. I noticed her perfectly painted nails and instinctively hid my hands behind my back. I couldn't remember the last time I had my nails done. "She finally left the sushi guys alone, and I haven't seen her harassing anybody else."

"Annabelle Archer!" A shrill voice came from above us.

"I spoke too soon." Kate fumbled with her shoes as she tried to wedge her feet back in them. We all turned around to greet Mrs. Pierce as she barreled unsteadily down the stairs toward us, a mass of overly bouffant blond hair and turquoise chiffon.

"Lord have mercy, she's drunk as a skunk!" Richard scurried out of her way. She plowed past us, pulling me by the sleeve as she went.

"I have some additional changes to make in the seating." Her words slurred as she staggered against the tables, craning to read the names on each place card. I averted my eyes at the mass of wrinkled cleavage barely contained by her strapless gown as she leaned over.

"The invitation clearly said 'black tie,' but there are some women here in pants, if you can imagine the nerve." She cut her eyes to me and appraised my outfit. "Of course it doesn't matter what you wear because you're just the help, but I won't have shabby guests sitting near my table."

"You want to change the names around now?" I felt a wave of panic begin to rise as I looked at my watch.

"Change names?" Mrs. Pierce paused then gave a harsh laugh. "Yes, that's exactly right. There will be plenty of name changing at this wedding. The ambassador does not go at this seat . . ."

"But Mrs. Pierce." I cringed as she knocked a water glass over. "The cocktail hour ends in ten minutes and the guests have already picked up their table cards. I'm sorry, but it's too late . . ."

Clara Pierce stopped me with a sharp snap of her fingers and turned to face me. I could feel my face begin to burn. After staring at me for a few seconds, she produced her notebook with a flourish and scrawled my name on the top page.

"You've turned out to be a great disappointment, Miss Archer. We'll discuss this matter later." She zigzagged her way back up the staircase.

"How much longer until it's all over?" I asked Kate, squeezing my hands into tight fists by my side.

"Four hours and six minutes, to be exact."

"Don't worry about it, Annie." Richard patted my

arm. "She's so drunk she probably won't remember a thing tomorrow morning."

Kate punched a fist into her open palm. "I'd love to beat her to death with that tiny notebook of hers."

"That would take forever." I picked up a votive candle that Mrs. Pierce had doused with water and sighed.

"That's the whole point, sugar." Richard winked at me. "Now I've got to go check on the kitchen. We're supposed to invite guests downstairs in five. Are we still on schedule?"

I managed a smile. "Always."

"Good." Richard started down the stairs. "I'll tell the chef."

"Do you have your itinerary?" I asked Kate when Richard walked out of earshot. "I think I lost mine again."

Kate rolled her eyes.

"I know, I know. I always leave my schedule lying around." I searched my pockets. "I remember having it during the family portrait session in the Salon Dore."

"The room in the back that looks like it's been hosed down in gold foil?" Kate started downstairs. "Well, let's go get it before the guests start coming down for dinner."

"We'll go through the rear galleries. It's faster and we don't have to push past all the waiters." I started walking up the staircase and stopped so Kate could catch up. "I can't wait until this night is over."

"You say that at every wedding!" Kate followed me

up the stairs toward the back galleries.

"But this time I really mean it, Kate." I reached a hand up to rub my neck. "I don't care how high-profile this wedding is anymore. It's not worth it!"

"If we survived melting wax to seal three hundred envelopes with the Pierce family crest, we can take a few more hours of this." Kate held up the finger I'd accidentally poured hot wax all over.

"Sorry about that," I said. Kate put an arm around my shoulder as we reached the landing between the foyer and the upper level. I could see that the cocktail hour was in full swing above us. The sound of the Dixieland jazz group we'd flown up from New Orleans could barely be heard over the din of the crowd. Body-to-body guests. Almost everyone in black. A typical Washington wedding.

"We never did talk about workman's comp," she continued as I raised my eyebrows. "All I'm asking for is one Friday night off to go out on a real weekend date."

"With the congressional aide?" I found it difficult to keep track of Kate's social life.

"No, I'm off politics for a while. This one's a lobbyist."

"How do you meet all these men?" Kate's ability to put in a sixty-hour workweek and still have an active social life amazed me. I felt lucky if I had time to water my plants.

"I don't find them," Kate shrugged, grinning. "They find me."

"Oh, right. I forgot you're the innocent bystander." I started to walk through the rotunda at the top of the landing. The lights in the back of the museum were turned off to discourage guests from wandering, and the room got dimmer as we walked. "Okay, I'll run next week's rehearsal, and you can take the night off."

"You're the greatest!" Kate hurried behind me. "I'll cover for you one night, if you ever want to go out."

"That's a pretty safe offer."

"Are you sure we should be going this way?" Kate held onto my sleeve. "The statue back here always gives me the creeps."

"I think when it's this expensive they call it a sculpture."

Kate ignored my comment. "Why don't you let me introduce you to someone? How about the assistant to the assistant of the White House chief of staff? He's too tame for me, but he'd be perfect for you."

"Thanks, Kate, but I'm too busy to get involved with anyone."

We reached the top of the staircase that led down to more of the back galleries and each held on to one of the side railings as we descended.

"Who said anything about getting involved?" Kate's clicking heels were like sonar pings on the dimly lit stairs.

"Then I'm definitely too busy!"

"Come on, Annabelle, you haven't been out with anyone since that doctor who moved to Algeria last year."

"Armenia."

"Close enough."

"They're not even on the same continent!"

We reached a small landing, and I could make out the final few stairs barely illuminated by the red and blue glow of a stained-glass window on display.

"We're going to kill ourselves." Kate started down ahead of me, then let out a small scream as she went sprawling off the last step and onto the floor.

"Are you hurt?" I knelt down next to her, my concern mixed with slight vindication that her absurdly high heels had finally gotten the best of her.

"I think I'm going to be sick."

"It can't be that bad, Kate. You probably just twisted your ankle."

"No, not that. I mean *her.*" She pointed behind me, and I turned to see a woman's body crumpled at the bottom of the stairs.

The woman's neck twisted so sharply that, even though she lay on her stomach, I could see the contorted wide-eyed expression on her face glowing in a mottled pattern of red and blue light from the stained glass.

Oh, God. I never meant it. Though I'd wished for it more times than I could remember over the past year, I'd never imagined it would happen.

The mother of the bride was dead.

18

Chapter 2

I pulled Kate to her feet as a waiter appeared at the top of the stairs.

"Get Richard," I called out. My mouth felt numb. "And make sure no guests come down here." Kate and I walked slowly up to the landing.

"Go ahead, Kate. I'll wait for Richard."

"I'm not going to leave you here." Kate motioned behind us. "With *her*."

"Just make sure nobody else comes back this way. We don't want to start a panic."

Kate paused, and I gave her a push. "Go on, and find a light switch."

She started shakily toward the main staircase, where guests began to filter downstairs for dinner. I watched her fumble along the wall and find the switch for the ambient lighting recessed high in the ceiling. It gave the room a dim glow. Better than being in the dark, at least.

When Richard appeared, Kate whispered something to him and he hurried toward me.

"What's Kate babbling about? What's going on? Who hit a big one?"

I half groaned, half laughed. "I think she meant 'bit the big one.'" I wondered if I'd ever heard Kate get an expression right. I motioned to the body at the foot of the stairs below me.

"Good heavens!"

"We found her just like that." I concentrated on speaking clearly as I felt my head start to pound. "What are we going to do?"

"Are you sure she's dead?" Richard didn't make a move toward going downstairs to check.

"Have you ever seen someone's neck do that?"

"We have to call the police," Richard shuddered and took his tiny silver cell phone out of his pocket.

"But the wedding . . ." I said. "All those people . . . the bride . . ."

"Annabelle." Richard grabbed me by the shoulders. "This isn't something we can fix with your emergency kit, and we certainly can't hide her."

"Nobody uses this staircase, anyway . . ."

"If you think we can carry on an entire wedding with the bride's mother lying spread-eagled on a back stairway, you're out of your mind! What are we supposed to do? Throw a tablecloth over her?"

"You're brilliant!" I ran past Kate and up the stairs to the cocktail area. I pulled an ivory damask linen off the nearest cocktail table and went back downstairs.

"You're not serious?" Richard stared at me.

"Come on." I started down the back staircase toward Mrs. Pierce. "I need help covering her."

"I'll have no part of this," Richard followed me down and stood on the last step with his hands on his hips. I unfurled the cloth over Mrs. Pierce and let it float down over her sprawled limbs.

"Damn," I said. "It's too small. We'll need one of the

20

bigger linens from the dining tables. Do you have any extras?"

Richard folded his arms over his chest and shook his head. "No, and don't even think of using my hand-beaded silk cloths, either. They cost me a fortune to get cleaned."

"Okay, then, we'll have to make do," I tugged the fabric over one of her feet and it slipped off her head. "Can you fix your side? It's all twisted."

"I'm calling the police." Richard snatched the table-cloth off Mrs. Pierce and marched up the stairs. "Unless you want to set up a champagne fountain over her?"

"Wait." I started to protest, then stopped. My shoulders sagged. "I'm not sure what got into me."

"You can't help it." Richard flipped open his phone. "It's the wedding planner in you."

I listened to his side of the conversation with the emergency dispatcher. After hanging up, he led me away from the stairs to Kate.

"I'll stay here until the police come, and make sure no one sees the body," Richard said. "Annabelle, you're going to have to tell the family before they see the paramedics arrive."

"This just keeps getting worse and worse."

"I'll go downstairs and wait for the police," Kate said.

"Let's go." Taking a deep breath, I fixed a smile on my face as Kate and I made our way down to the foyer.

Guests stood milling around the tables, apparently

continuing the cocktail reception from upstairs. I spotted the bride and groom near the dance floor as Kate headed for the front entrance.

The groom had his arm secured around the bride's waist and both were smiling, the bride gazing adoringly at her husband whenever he spoke.

I hadn't gotten very close to the bride or the groom while planning their wedding. As a matter of fact, I'd only met them a handful of times. Safe to say Clara Pierce hadn't liked to share the decision-making process.

My eyes rested on the bride. Elizabeth was a sweet, Barbie-doll blond girl as placid and easygoing as her mother had been argumentative and difficult. Usually mother-daughter wedding planning could be counted on for at least one tearful exchange, but Elizabeth had never objected to her mother's firm handling of the wedding. I'd never seen the two argue. Kate had claimed once, with some amount of disdain, that the girl was too lovestruck to notice anything. Easy to see why.

Dr. Andrew Donovan was everything a woman, or her social-climbing mother, could dream of. Tall and darkly handsome, the young doctor had an intoxicating smile and an Ivy League pedigree that satisfied even his future mother-in-law's hunger for status. After hearing Mrs. Pierce extol his virtues for nearly a year, I wasn't sure whether Elizabeth or her mother loved him more.

"Excuse me, Dr. Donovan." I touched his sleeve to

get his attention. He stared at me blankly for a moment, and then bestowed one of those famous smiles on me.

"The wedding planner!" he said loudly to the group around him. "Hasn't she done a fabulous job?"

"Thank you." I tried to make my voice sound natural. "May I speak with you for a moment?"

"Is anything wrong?" The bride tore her gaze away from her husband's perfect features.

"Of course not, dear. What could be wrong?" The groom answered before I had a chance to speak. "I'll be back before you can miss me." He kissed her on the nose, and then followed me to the middle of the dance floor, where no guests could overhear.

"There's been an accident," I tried to get the words out as fast as possible. "Mrs. Pierce fell down a flight of stairs." When he didn't respond immediately, I continued. "She's dead."

The doctor put a hand over his eyes.

"Where is she?" He pulled his hand away from his face. "Maybe I can help."

Before I could answer him, two uniformed policemen arrived, and I watched Kate direct them upstairs. The crowd buzzed with curious chatter and a few people tried to get past Kate to follow the police.

"Andrew!" Elizabeth ran up to her new husband and clutched his arm. "What's happening? Why are the police here?"

The groom put his arms around her, and I turned away. Wouldn't it be better if she heard it from him

23

than from me? I didn't want to have to see her face when she found out her mother was dead and her wedding ruined. Knowing brides the way I did, I couldn't be sure which would upset her more.

I pushed through the crowd of wedding guests and headed toward the front door. I needed fresh air.

"Whoa, there, ma'am."

I'd run headlong into a man in a wrinkled, blue button-down shirt. Obviously not a wedding guest.

"Sorry." I stepped back, sizing him up. Dark hair, broad shoulders, and hazel-brown eyes that held mine without faltering. I sucked in my breath. Wow.

"Are you in charge here?" He'd apparently given me the once-over and then decided that I didn't look like a wedding guest, either.

"Well, I'm the wedding planner, so I guess . . ."

"I'm Detective Mike Reese." He held out his hand and I shook it. "You're the one who found the body, right?"

"My assistant and I both found her. My name's Annabelle Archer."

The detective nodded. "Your assistant already spoke to one of my officers. Would you mind coming back to the body with me? I have a few questions for you."

I followed him up the stairs to the back galleries. The sculptures that were so eerie in the dark seemed harmless with all the lights on. Detective Reese led me to the rear stairway and down to the middle landing. Several uniformed officers blocked the remaining stairs and another snapped pictures of the entire area. I waited at the landing while the detective went down the staircase and knelt beside the body. Two men in tuxedos followed a police officer down to the body and began examining it. One of the advantages to having lots of doctors as guests. A few minutes later, the paramedics rushed by me down the stairs.

Mrs. Pierce hadn't improved any since we'd last seen her. The blue of her dress cast a purplish hue on her skin and her contorted mouth had become pale and waxy.

"Not bad looking," Kate walked up to me.

"What?"

"He's hot." Kate pointed at Detective Reese. "Who is he?"

"A detective."

"You know, I've never dated a cop," Kate watched the officers working around her. "There are some cute ones here, too."

"And here I viewed this whole 'mother of the bride dying' as a negative thing." Kate didn't hear me. She'd wandered over to talk to one of the officers. My next assistant would be a little old lady with cataracts.

"Annie." Richard hurried up to me. "I've been searching all over for you."

"I'm waiting to be questioned by the detective." I motioned to the only person clustered around the body not in a uniform.

"Well, lucky you," Richard gave me a nudge, and then became serious again. "I'm not sure if I can keep these guests calm much longer. They want to know what's going on."

"Have you told them anything?"

"Well, I couldn't exactly make an announcement that their hostess is twisted up like a human pretzel, now could I?"

"I'll have one of my men make an appropriate announcement." The detective joined our conversation. He turned to Richard. "You must be the caterer who placed the 911 call."

Richard winked at me. "Well, we know why you made detective so young."

Detective Reese ignored Richard's comment. He wore latex gloves and flipped open a small notepad. "We found this on the body. Do either of you have any idea what these names and notes mean?"

"Those are Mrs. Pierce's recorded infractions." My stomach tightened at the sight of the familiar spiral notepad. "She always had it with her."

"Infractions?" The detective looked confused.

"Mrs. Pierce was . . . how would you put it? Well, particular about the way things were done." Richard gestured to the notebook with a wave of his hands. "If she didn't like what someone did, she would write their name down in that notebook. We called it her 'hit list.'"

"Interesting." Detective Reese glanced up at Richard. "What did she mean by writing the words 'skewers too sharp' next to your name?"

"Oh, heavens." Richard tossed his head back in a

manufactured laugh. "She wanted me to dull the skewers I used on the Indonesian satay station so she wouldn't poke herself in the roof of her mouth."

"Did you?"

"Have you ever seen a blunt skewer?" Richard tapped his foot on the ground. "Defeats the purpose."

"Who's Maxwell Gray?" The detective turned to another page in the notebook. "And how would he have 'taken the wrong side?'"

"The photographer." I noticed that my palms were getting sweaty, and I tried to wipe them on my pants without anyone noticing. "Mrs. Pierce was compulsive about being photographed from her right. She had me remind him a dozen times."

"So what did you do to upset her?" Detective Reese's eyes met mine as he opened to the page where Mrs. Pierce had written my name in big, scrawling letters.

"I wouldn't let her rearrange the guest's table assignments at the last minute."

"I'm afraid I'm not following."

"She felt that some guests weren't dressed well enough, so she wanted them moved to the back."

"Naturally." Detective Reese cleared his throat. "When did this altercation between you two occur?"

"It couldn't have been more than ten minutes before we found her." I picked at a loose thread on the sleeve of my jacket. "But I wouldn't call it an altercation. I mean, she was pretty drunk, so I didn't take it too seriously."

The detective's eyes widened. "She appeared drunk

when you last saw her?"

"The woman could barely stand up." Richard leaned close to the detective and gave him a nudge. "I'm surprised she could remember Annabelle's name, let alone write it down."

Reese turned to me and took a small step away from Richard. "Did you see her argue with anyone else tonight?"

"My assistant, Kate, mentioned that Mrs. Pierce had an issue with the sushi chefs, but I don't think it was serious."

"Why all the interest in the hit list?" Richard rested a hand on the detective's arm and lowered his voice. "Do you suspect foul play?"

"Just getting all the information." Reese returned Mrs. Pierce's notebook to the plastic evidence bag and backed away from us. "Excuse me for a second."

"He seems nice." Richard's eyes followed the detective. "Don't you think, Annabelle?"

"Richard." I grabbed him by the shoulders. "He's a cop."

"I know."

"Nice or not, I get the feeling he considers us suspects."

"Why would he even be thinking this is anything but an accident?" Richard readjusted his shirt collar. "The woman was clearly drunk and took a spill down the stairs. End of story."

"Not exactly." Kate walked up and motioned for us to follow her away from the group of nearby police officers. When we moved out of earshot, she lowered her voice to a whisper. "They think it may not have been an accident."

"How do you know?" Richard's face drained of color, despite all the hours he'd put in at the tanning salon.

"Do you see that cute uniformed officer?"

Richard stared over my shoulder. "Mr. Biceps?"

"Wait." I held up my hands. "Let me guess where this story is going."

"We were having a nice little chat until another officer pulled him away." Kate kept her voice low. "I overheard them talking about an odd rash that the doctors who tried to revive her found. The ME will most likely do a tox screening."

"The ME?"

"Medical examiner, Annabelle," Kate sounded exasperated. "The guy with the body now. Get with the program."

"They think a rash killed her?" Richard made a face. "What a horrible way to go."

I groaned. Kate wasn't always the most reliable source of information. Especially if it came from a man.

"She didn't die from a rash." Kate looked at us as if we were idiots. "You guys aren't the brightest balls in the box, are you?"

"Does she mean brightest bulbs?" Richard asked me out of the corner of his mouth.

Kate ignored him. "The rash apparently would've

been caused by a medication overdose."

"So she overdosed on Valium or something." Richard shrugged his shoulders. "Not surprising in this crowd."

"That's not what the police are saying." Kate shifted her gaze from Richard to me. "They're saying this might have been intentional."

"Murder?" Richard went completely white and leaned back against the wall, his hand clasped against his heart.

"Murder." Kate nodded vigorously. "Poison."

Richard gave a tiny gasp before going limp and sliding down to the floor.

Chapter 3

"I'm absolutely mortified," Richard spoke into my answering machine as it began to record. I fumbled to pick up the cordless phone next to my bed.

"I told you a hundred times last night, it's no big deal," I said into the receiver, my voice still scratchy. "I felt like fainting myself."

"Do you know how bad it makes me look?"

"Hardly anyone saw you."

"Annabelle, I'm not talking about what I looked like slumped against the wall. It makes me look like the prime suspect."

"You're just being paranoid." I sat up in bed and saw the suit I'd left crumpled on the floor after stepping out of it the night before. "Why would your fainting spell have anything to do with being a suspect?"

"Oh, God, Annabelle. Don't call it a 'fainting spell.' You make me sound like one of those Southern belles who wore their corsets too tight."

"Good thinking. You can explain to the police that your corset was too tight."

"You're an absolute joy in the morning." The sarcasm dripped from his voice.

"It's not morning anymore." I picked up my alarm clock and groaned. Daylight poured into the dark room as I opened the blinds next to my bed. "Why are you so obsessed about this, anyway?"

"Do you know why I had to close my restaurant?"

"That happened before I knew you," I reminded him.

"Food poisoning." Richard let out a long breath. "Imagine what it felt like to hear the word 'poison' bandied about again."

"That's why you fainted? Well, food poisoning is totally different from murder. Nobody's going to blame you for this one."

"Hearing anything associated with poison is never good for a caterer." Richard's voice became shrill. "You know how people in this industry talk, Annabelle. They're going to have a field day with this."

"You're right about that." I walked from my bedroom to my office and flipped on the light. Small Tiffany-blue favor boxes for my next wedding covered the floor, so I leaned into the room as far as I could and craned to see the phone on my desk. I moved a mound of pastel file folders out of the way and could see the business line's answering-machine display blinking red. "I have seventeen new messages since yesterday, and it's barely two o'clock."

"No doubt all concerned colleagues," Richard muttered.

"Concerned with getting the dirt, you mean." I pulled the door shut and continued down the hall to the kitchen, promising myself that I would spend some quality time cleaning my office. Soon.

Richard gave a deep sigh. "I'm sure all the other caterers are celebrating my demise as we speak."

"What are you talking about? You weren't the one murdered." I turned on the fluorescent kitchen lights and opened the refrigerator door. A package of fat-free cheese slices, a browning head of lettuce, and a nearly empty plastic bottle of Diet Dr Pepper. I added grocery shopping to my mental to-do list.

"Might as well have been," Richard moaned. "Once the word is out that a guest died at one of my events, the clients won't be lining up."

"Stop being so melodramatic. The detective said that they'd know more about the cause of death in a day or two. They'll find out that your food had nothing to do with it, and you'll be totally cleared."

"A day or two! I won't have any clients left in a day or two."

"Listen." I rolled my eyes and poured the remaining soda into a glass. I took a big swallow. Completely flat.

I made a face and took another drink. "There's nothing we can do except wait until the police have finished their investigation."

"Aren't you the least bit curious about who murdered that horror of a woman?"

"It would be nice to know who to thank."

"Annabelle," he scolded me. "You have no respect for the dead."

"Come off it. I'm not going to pretend that I liked the woman. Okay, I'm sorry someone killed her. Not a nice thing to do, but if anyone had it coming . . ."

"I wouldn't go around saying that since you were the last person to argue with her before she died."

"Whose side are you on, Richard?" My old-fashioned doorbell rang loudly. I put the glass down on the counter and hurried down the hall to my bedroom.

"Is that your door? Probably the press wanting an interview. I told you this wedding would put you in the spotlight."

"It's probably someone trying to sell something." I grabbed my suit pants from the floor of my room and pulled them on, then threw on the jacket and buttoned it up. No one would ever guess I didn't have anything on underneath.

"Whoever it is, they really want to talk to you if they climbed four flights of stairs. You'd think they'd have more elevators in an area like Georgetown."

"That's why it's called a walk-up, Richard, and it's supposed to be charming." I walked down the hall to the front door.

"Exhausting, is what it is."

"I've gotta go. Try not to poison anyone today." I clicked off the phone as I swung open the door. "Detective Reese!"

I fumbled to put the phone down on the bookshelf next to me. My first-floor neighbor, Leatrice Butters, stood next to him smiling. A tiny woman in her late seventies, she never left her apartment without a heavy dose of bright coral lipstick and her unnaturally dark hair curled up in a Mary Tyler Moore flip. She wore a multicolored striped blouse and matching hand-painted sneakers, which I recognized as one of her gardening outfits.

"I went outside to check on the tulip beds, and found this nice young man on his way to see you." Leatrice took Reese's hand and squeezed past me into the apartment.

Leatrice noticed the mounds of papers on the dining room table and the books in towering piles on the floor. She shook her head. "She's a busy career woman. No time for anything but work."

"Thank you, Leatrice." I tried to keep my voice pleasant as I closed the door.

"I'll make us all some coffee while you entertain your guest." Leatrice ignored my protests and hurried to the kitchen. "Happy to do it, dear. Happy to do it."

"Nice place." Reese sat down on my yellow, overstuffed couch. I pulled back the front drapes and light flooded the sparsely furnished room. I moaned inwardly as I noticed the herds of dust bunnies on my hardwood floors.

"Thanks, but it's a mess." I straightened a pile of wedding magazines on the coffee table. "As my very helpful neighbor told you, I've been swamped with work."

Detective Reese leaned forward and picked up one of the pink candy hearts that were piled in a bowl next to the magazines. "I thought these were only around at Valentine's Day."

"Those are special ones we got with the bride's and groom's names printed on them. We had a lot left over that they didn't want." I didn't add that I snacked on them constantly and had seriously considered ordering a private batch when I ran out.

He popped it into his mouth. "Pretty creative. So you plan weddings full time?"

"Full time and then some." I swept my hair out of my face and let it fall down my back. "Brides are pretty demanding clients."

"Mrs. Pierce more than most, I take it?"

"You asked me these questions last night, Detective. Why are you questioning me a second time?" I suddenly noticed that my suit was covered in beige lint from the area rug in my bedroom, and I felt my face flush. Fabulous. It looked as though I'd been rolling around on the floor.

"I thought you might be able to help me out." He smiled as his eyes traveled down my crumpled outfit. I hadn't remembered that he had dimples, too.

"Sure." I sat down across from him in the yellow twill chair that matched the couch, trying to brush off some of the lint on my suit without being obvious. Still grinning, he took a notebook out of his blazer pocket.

"We made a list of the guests in the Corcoran last night, but I wondered if you might have an original guest list."

"I have the list of names and addresses we gave to the calligrapher." I went over to the dining room table and shuffled through the folders to find it. I couldn't remember the last time I'd actually eaten at that table. "What are you hoping to find?"

"There's a name in the victim's notepad we can't match up with any of the guests or staff at the reception."

I located the thick list of names and handed it to Reese. "She didn't limit her infractions to the wedding."

"I'm guessing that some of her guests declined the invitation and got themselves written up." He gave me a quick wink, and then began studying the list.

"It sounds like you're catching on to Mrs. Pierce's style, Detective."

"Thanks." He held my gaze for a second before returning to the papers. I hadn't remembered his eyes having so much green in them. Not that it mattered.

"Coffee's ready." Leatrice walked into the room carrying a wicker tray with three mismatched mugs and set it on my glass coffee table. "You don't have a thing to eat in there, Annabelle."

"I'm never here to eat," I said, more to Reese than to her. Why did I feel that I needed to explain myself?

"So how did you two meet?" Leatrice handed us both a mug and perched on the couch. She leaned closer to Reese as he started to take a drink. "I already added some sugar and there isn't any milk to be found."

"We met last night when one of my clients died at the wedding." I watched Leatrice's face drop. "Detective Reese is in charge of the case."

"I'm here to get some more information from Ms. Archer."

"Heavens!" Leatrice put her hand over her mouth and shook her head back and forth. Then her eyes lit up. "A murder case?"

"We're exploring all the possibilities." Reese flipped through the guest list, his eyes darting from the paper to Leatrice. "It's not as exciting as it sounds, ma'am."

"I read mystery novels all the time." Leatrice took a sip of her coffee. "I'm always on the lookout for suspicious people. Isn't that right, Annabelle?"

"Any luck with the name?" I tried to steer the conversation back to Reese's investigation before Leatrice could launch into a lengthy chat about her methods of neighborhood surveillance.

He shook his head. "Does the name Phillips mean anything to you?"

"Not really." I picked up a stray rubber band on the coffee table and pulled my hair back into a ponytail. "Aside from the Phillips Collection."

He raised an eyebrow. "The art gallery?"

"Right. But I don't think Mrs. Pierce had any connections to it."

"It's worth checking out." He stood up to leave.

Leatrice jumped up after him. "You should check out all leads, Detective. You never know what might turn up."

"Yes, ma'am, you're absolutely right." Reese turned to me. "Do you mind if I keep this list? I'll return it to you once we're done."

"No need to return it to me."

"Thanks, but I may have to return to ask you more questions, anyway." Reese walked toward the door.

"Come back any time." Leatrice followed him.

"Thanks for the coffee." He handed his mug to Leatrice, who blushed as she held open the door. She didn't close it until he'd walked halfway down the stairs.

"Isn't he charming?" Leatrice headed for the kitchen with Reese's mug. "And so handsome."

"Don't even try, Leatrice." I warned her. "He's not my type."

"I didn't know you had a type, dear."

"Well if I did have a type, it wouldn't be a cop." I rubbed my clammy palms on the legs of my pantsuit.

"Not fancy enough for you?" Leatrice returned to the living room.

"That's not it." I grabbed a handful of sugar hearts and tossed one in my mouth.

"Well, he's better than those young hotshots you bring around every so often. All those boys care about is their careers."

"How do you know?" I'd never let her know how

right she was. I hadn't had the best luck with Washington men.

"I told you, I'm very observant. Comes from reading those detective novels."

The phone's high-pitched ring made me jump. I grabbed it from the bookshelf.

"Annabelle." Richard's voice crackled on the other end. He was on his cell phone.

"Where are you? I can barely hear you."

"I'm in the closet."

"What are you talking about?" I pressed the phone closer to my ear.

"I'm hiding in here so no one can hear me," Richard whispered.

"Who's going to hear you?"

"You've got to help me." Richard's voice faded in and out. "It's a matter of life or death."

Chapter 4

"For your information, a cocktail party for twenty does not constitute a life or death situation." I stood in the kitchen of one of Richard's clients, breathing hard from running the five blocks from my apartment. Richard barely glanced at me as he placed cookie sheets along the counter.

"It does for a caterer who's on the brink of extinction. This is the only client who hasn't fired me, and I'm not about to let her down."

"So where do I come into all this? I hope you didn't make me run all the way here just to have someone to complain to."

"Why didn't you drive?" Richard sounded impatient.

"And try to find a new parking space in Georgetown on the weekend? The closest spot would have been more than five blocks away."

"Did you bring a black skirt and white blouse?"

I nodded and pulled the items out of my red nylon bag—a designer knockoff I'd bought from a street vendor. "I followed your orders precisely, Commander. What's this about, anyway?"

"As you're fully aware, I couldn't hire any staff for tonight. I'm technically supposed to be shut down until this murder business is cleared up."

"You don't think I'm going to play cocktail waitress for your illicit party, do you?"

"Fine, you don't have to be a cocktail waitress." Richard placed miniature beef Wellingtons on cookie sheets in perfectly spaced rows. "We'll call you the food-and-beverage distribution engineer."

"Hilarious." I took the white apron he handed me and tied it around my waist. "You owe me one."

"We'll consider it payback for your client who had me place garden gnomes on the buffets at her wedding."

"That happened three years ago." I put my hands on my hips. "I can't believe you're still upset about that."

Richard narrowed his eyes at me. "Are you forgetting that I had to dress the gnomes to match the wedding party?"

"Okay, but after tonight we're even."

Richard nodded. "I've been doing parties for this client for years. They like to keep things simple, which is lucky for us."

"So what's the timing?"

"Since it's a pretheater cocktail reception, guests will start arriving at six-thirty and they'll all leave by eight to make it to the Kennedy Center."

"Then we've got plenty of time." I relaxed and hopped up onto a kitchen stool.

"Not quite." Richard motioned me off the stool with a jerk of his head. "Dr. and Mrs. Henderson like to make surprise inspections of the setup."

"Henderson . . . that name sounds familiar. Have you mentioned them to me before?"

"Maybe I did because they live so close to you."

"I've always wondered who lives in this house." I pushed the swinging door to the dining room open and peeked out. "I can see the front room lit up at night when I walk by. The artwork is gorgeous."

"They spent a fortune renovating the place." Richard lowered his voice to a conspiratorial whisper. "The moldings alone took three months to get right."

"Is it okay if I take a peek around?" I gave Richard puppy-dog eyes, and he groaned.

"Only if you make it snappy. We've got four dozen wild mushroom chopsticks to wrap, fifty Brie tartlets to fill . . ."

I let the kitchen door swing closed before Richard could recite the entire menu. The noise of my heels on the hardwood floors sounded deafening, so I slipped out of my shoes and padded in my bare feet from the dining room into the front parlor. A polished black grand piano covered with framed photographs stood in front of the expansive bay window. Dr. and Mrs. Henderson at a black tie party, Dr. and Mrs. Henderson on a sailboat with a group of friends, Dr. and Mrs. Henderson with a pretty blonde in a graduation cap. I looked at the photo on the boat again, then picked it up and walked back to the kitchen.

"You didn't tell me that the Hendersons are friends with the Pierces." I waved the silver frame in front of Richard.

"Dr. Henderson is in the same practice as Dr. Pierce. Isn't the groom in with them, as well?"

"No, he joined Clara's ex-husband's practice right after we were hired, remember?"

Richard nodded. "Now I do. Our MOB wasn't too thrilled."

"Were the Hendersons at the wedding?"

"Most definitely. Mrs. Henderson wore that silver backless dress that Kate drooled over all night."

I put the picture down and rubbed my temples. "This can't be good."

"What's the problem, Annabelle?"

"Catering a party against police orders the day after one of our clients gets killed is one thing, but doing it for a group of witnesses and friends of the victim is another."

"Relax." Richard handed me a mound of dough and

42

a rolling pin. "Rolling out some dough for the mushroom chopsticks will help you take your mind off things."

"Nice try. Let me put this picture back before someone misses it." I tiptoed to the parlor and replaced the frame. Before I could turn around, I heard a series of fast, clicking footsteps coming down the stairs.

"Of course we're still having the party." I assumed this low, cultured voice belonged to Mrs. Henderson. "Why on earth would we cancel just because of last night?"

I searched the room to find a place to hide. In a few seconds she'd be standing in front of me and I'd have to explain why I was wandering around her house barefoot. Not a good first impression. My eyes rested on the billowy blue curtains that pooled on the floor. *Thank God sheers are out this season,* I thought as I slipped behind the heavy drapes.

Mrs. Henderson came into the room. I could hear pacing. "Yes, it's the same caterer and no, you have nothing to worry about."

She must be talking on the phone to one of her guests for tonight's party. I shifted my weight so I didn't lean against the window. I could imagine crashing through the glass and landing outside in the bushes.

"Of course I'm sure Richard Gerard didn't have anything to do with her death."

I heard some voices outside. I pivoted my body toward the window and realized that everyone who walked by on the sidewalk could see me cowering behind the curtains that covered the bay window. Like most houses in Georgetown, this one sat so close to the sidewalk that people could almost touch it as they passed. *Please let no one I know see me.*

"Because I know who did kill her, that's why."

My heart started pounding. I couldn't believe Mrs. Henderson was talking about the murderer.

"I didn't see anything, but it doesn't take a genius to figure out who wanted her dead," Mrs. Henderson said in an authoritative voice.

I felt a drop of sweat trickle down my neck as a man outside stopped to stare at me. I pretended to be wiping a spot on the glass and smiled at him. Perfectly natural to be cleaning the windows hunched over behind the curtains.

"I've got to go, hon." Mrs. Henderson's footsteps sounded as though they were in the foyer now. "Donald is running the water for my preparty bubble bath."

I waited until I heard her walk upstairs, then I dashed back to the kitchen, scooping up my shoes as I went.

"Where have you been?" Flour covered Richard's apron and most of the floor.

I waved his question away. "I just overheard your hostess talking about Mrs. Pierce's murderer."

"How did you overhear that?"

"I hid behind the living room curtains when she came downstairs," I mumbled.

Richard opened his mouth to speak, then shook his head.

I held up my hand. "Don't start with me."

"Okay, so did Mrs. Henderson say who killed the wicked witch?"

"No." I took the pile of linen napkins that Richard pushed toward me and started folding them. "She didn't mention a name."

"That doesn't do us much good, Watson."

"Why do I have to be Watson?" I sat on a stool and swung my bare feet in front of me.

"Elementary, my dear." Richard wagged an oven-mitted finger. "Holmes never cowered behind curtains to solve a crime."

"I'm not trying to solve anything, but it doesn't hurt for us to keep our ears open tonight," I insisted.

"As long as your investigation doesn't interfere with your ability to pass hors d'oeuvres."

"Just think, Richard," I finished folding the stack of napkins into neat squares and stepped into my black slingbacks as I stood up, "maybe one of the guests tonight will reveal the murderer."

"Maybe one of tonight's guests *is* the murderer."

I gulped hard as someone began rapping on the door.

Chapter 5

"The guests, or should I say suspects, are starting to arrive." I stuck my head in the kitchen door and Richard glared at me. "How do I look in my uniform?"

"Stunning. You've got to hold them off for a few

minutes. I still need to garnish." He shooed me away with a handful of parsley. "Take that tray of white wine with you."

I balanced the silver tray of filled wine glasses on my arm. "Perfect. The more they drink, the more they'll talk."

"I hardly think you're going to wiggle a confession out of someone with a precocious Pinot Grigio."

"I'll use what I've got." I winked at Richard. "God help us."

When I walked back to the living room several more couples had arrived. The sound of big band came from the piped-in stereo system, but the high-pitched chatter of women greeting each other masked the music. A group of men clustered around the display of antipasto I'd put out earlier. Mrs. Henderson held court in the center of the room in a sleek black dress, her dark hair piled on top of her head. She motioned me over with a flick of her fingers, and I hurried over to proffer my tray.

"You can imagine my shock." Mrs. Henderson turned back to her friends after taking a glass of wine. I stepped away from the group and hovered nearby, pretending to wipe a nonexistent spill from an end table.

One of the ladies leaned close and lowered her voice. "Did you actually see the body?"

"No," Mrs. Henderson said with some measure of disappointment. "But I saw a few things the police didn't."

"What do you mean?"

I held my breath and took a step closer.

Mrs. Henderson turned to face me. "How much longer until hors d'oeuvres are passed?"

"I'll go check." I hurried back into the kitchen.

"Good," Richard held out two glass trays edged in parsley and brightly colored edible flowers. "Let me explain what's on each one."

"No time to waste." I took the trays out of his hands and dashed out of the kitchen.

"Annabelle, get back here." Richard called after me. "You don't know what you're serving!"

I went back up to Mrs. Henderson with the trays in hand, trying not to breathe hard.

"Where was he when they found her?" One of the women asked Mrs. Henderson.

"Who knows? Probably with Bev Tripton. Try the Brie tarts."

"Her best friend? Do they have nuts in them?"

"Well?" Mrs. Henderson looked pointedly at me. "Do the Brie tarts have nuts in them?"

I glanced at the tray and tried to remember if I'd seen any nuts in the kitchen. I swallowed hard as the women stared at me, and my mouth went dry.

"No nuts."

"Good." The No-Nut lady popped the tart in her mouth. "If I so much as touch a nut, I have to go to the hospital."

Oh, God. I rushed back to the kitchen and slumped against the counter near Richard. I felt faint. "Please tell me the Brie things don't have nuts."

"I will not have my hors d'oeuvres referred to as things. They're Brie tartlets and, no, I left the nuts out this time. They do have a hint of saffron, though." Richard pulled off his oven mitts and raised an eyebrow. "Why?"

I motioned toward the party. "Nut allergy."

"I told you to wait for me to explain the food to you." Richard's face began to flush, and he threw the oven mitts down. "But, no. You had to run off and try to kill more of my clients."

"No harm done." I reached for one of the crab puffs that Richard had arranged on a hand-painted ceramic plate and he smacked my hand away. I jerked back and ducked out of the range of his swinging dish towel. "I think I overheard something important. Apparently someone had a liaison with Mrs. Pierce's best friend last night when the murder happened."

Richard barely concealed his disdain. "You call that a clue?"

"It has to be someone important. Someone who shouldn't have been with her."

"Like who, her husband?" Richard started to laugh, and then stopped. "It could have been her husband. Now things are getting interesting."

"So far it's just a theory."

"Well you're not going to find out by sitting in here." Richard handed the plate of crab puffs to me.

"You just want me to get back to work," I grumbled.

"I've always admired your keen perception, Annabelle." Richard pushed me out the door. "Now go!"

I made my way through the ever-growing crowd, spotting Mrs. Henderson and her friends in the far corner, huddled together. By the gleeful looks on their faces, I'd missed a color commentary of the murder. I tried to push my way through a group of men, holding the plate above my head.

"Of course he did it." A man with wide sideburns stared at the plate of hors d'oeuvres as it moved past him. "Wouldn't you have killed that woman?"

I spun on my heel and swung the tray down. "Crab puff?"

"No doubt he had a motive." A man wearing a plaid tie popped a puff into his mouth.

"Motive? She didn't give him a motive, she gave him a mandate."

"They're excellent with the remoulade sauce, sir."

"Trying to ruin his career just asked for trouble." Plaid Tie shifted his eyes to me. "I don't like spicy food, thank you."

"It's very mild," I assured him.

"He wouldn't have been foolish enough to actually kill her, though. She's right, Glen. The sauce is delicious."

"Maybe he didn't do it, but he should have." Sideburns jumped in the conversation. "I prefer old-fashioned tartar sauce myself."

"We'll probably never know if he did do it. He's much too smart to get caught. Do you have any tartar sauce, young lady?"

"I'm sure I can find some for you." I turned and raced to the kitchen.

Richard had arranged the remaining hors d'oeuvres on trays. "How did the crab puffs go over?"

"We've had a request for tartar sauce."

"Tartar sauce?" Richard shrieked. "Why don't I just slap a bunch of fish sticks on a plate and they can eat all the tartar sauce they want?"

"I thought you'd feel this way." I tried not to laugh as Richard threw open the refrigerator door and began rummaging through the contents.

Richard shook a fist in the air. "These are the same people that ask for A-1 with their filet mignon."

"What have you heard about Mrs. Pierce trying to ruin her husband's career?"

"Nothing." He slammed the refrigerator door shut. "Why would she do that?"

I tapped my fingers on the counter. "I'm not sure, but that's what the tartar-sauce guys were talking about."

"Are you sure they were talking about her husband?"

"I just assumed they were," I admitted. "But they never mentioned him by name."

"Knowing what we do of Clara Pierce, it's possible that more than one man had a reason to kill her. Pretty likely, as a matter of fact." Richard grimaced as he shook the contents of a plastic bottle. "Squeezable tartar sauce. What's this world coming to?"

Before I could respond, a crash of glass came from the living room. Richard jumped and squeezed the plastic bottle at the same time, sending an uneven stream of tartar sauce into the air.

Richard had bits of chunky sauce splattered on his face. Globs of white dotted the shiny copper pots hanging above him and dripped onto his head. I put my hand over my mouth to keep from laughing. "Well, now the only thing we need to make this party perfect is a dead body."

Richard narrowed his eyes. "The night's young, Annabelle."

Chapter 6

"Was that so hard?" Richard handed me the last wine glass to dry.

"Now I remember why I'm a wedding planner and not a caterer. At least I've never had to clean my clients' kitchens." I glanced around at the sparkling stainless-steel appliances and the dark granite counter-tops that were cleaner now than when I'd arrived. I could almost see my own reflection in the copper pots dangling above us. No evidence of the chaos that had taken place only an hour before and not a single drop of tartar sauce anywhere. I had to hand it to Richard. He could break down a party even faster than he could throw it together.

"I've always said you wedding planners were a bit soft."

"Soft?" My jaw dropped open. "Who cleaned up that

crystal bowl of artichoke dip that someone broke all over the living room floor?"

"I never said you weren't useful, honey."

"And did you see how much wine those people went through? I'm surprised they could still walk out the front door."

"I'm quite aware of how much wine they drank because I washed every last glass."

Richard picked up a red milk crate full of cooking utensils and trays, and I pushed open the heavy kitchen door that led out to the alley. When we reached the sidewalk, I looked around for his silver Mercedes convertible. Cars were lined up end to end along both sides of the street, inching over driveways and blatantly ignoring NO PARKING signs, but I didn't see Richard's car anywhere.

"Didn't you drive?"

"I tried, but the closest parking space I could find was the one I already had in front of my house." Richard shifted the milk crate onto his hip. "It's impossible to find parking on the weekend. Sometimes I wonder why I bother to live in Georgetown at all."

"You live here because it's fashionable," I reminded Richard before he launched into a laundry list of petty grievances.

"Well, there is that." Richard began walking in the opposite direction of his house toward my building. "Come on, I'll walk you home."

I knew it would be a waste of breath to argue. Living in a city hadn't affected Richard's sense of chivalry

one bit. Anyway, he loved strolling around Georgetown at night and peeking into all the fabulously decorated row houses. "Window shopping," he called it.

"Where else in the city can you find homes like
this?" He motioned with an elbow at a house with two
ornate iron staircases leading up to a pair of lampposts.

"Mm-hmm." I alternated between looking up at the
house and watching the uneven brick sidewalk. "Who
do you think those men at the party were talking about,
anyway?"

"The house on the next block is really something to
talk about. Wait until you see the chandelier in the front
room and the fresco on the outside."

"We already know that her current husband may
have been having an affair and couldn't be found
during the wedding, so don't you think that gives him
motive and opportunity?"

"I wouldn't be surprised if it's Waterford, though."
Richard ignored the taxi at the intersection, and I hurried across the street after him. "They have money,
even if they don't have restraint."

"It could have been anyone. Everyone wanted to kill
her. Even we wanted to kill her." I stumbled over a bit
of tree root that poked through the sidewalk. "All we
have to do is sort out the motives."

"Talk about too much!" Richard gazed up at a brick
house with an enormous crystal chandelier dominating
the yellow living room. The front room was almost
entirely windows and the lights were on, giving us a
perfect view. "Palladian windows weren't enough for

them. They had to do double Palladian."

"Considering her winning personality, I think our prime suspects should be the people who knew her best." I tugged Richard by the sleeve, and we resumed walking. "Which brings us back to her current husband, who may or may not have been having an affair."

I ran the short list of suspects through my head as we turned up the next street.

"Sometimes you just wonder what people were thinking," Richard gasped.

"I know," I agreed, trying to imagine who could have committed murder. "It's awful."

"It's beyond awful." Richard pointed at a white lattice carport dripping with vines. "It's like the Hanging Gardens of Babylon right here in Georgetown. Have you ever seen anything like it?"

"I've never seen anything as awful as Mrs. Pierce's mangled body. But if the fall wasn't what killed her . . . if that rash on her neck means she may have been poisoned, then the killer didn't have to push her down the stairs. Anyone Mrs. Pierce came in contact with during the night could have murdered her."

"Now that's a real crime." Richard nodded at two enormous urns that flanked a doorway. They were ornamented with carved floral swags spilling down the front.

"A crime of passion isn't out of the question." I shrugged. "Especially if Mrs. Pierce found out about the affair. Let's not forget the ex-husband, either. I have no doubt she made their divorce as painful as possible. So I'd say those are our two prime suspects."

"You have to have both, I suppose." Richard shuddered and made a face. "It would be off-balance to have just one."

"I never thought about it that way, Richard, but they could've been working together. Why not? More than one killer makes a lot of sense."

Richard stopped short as we rounded the corner onto my street, and I bumped into him. "Are you expecting another visit from the police, Annabelle?"

I followed his gaze and saw a pair of squad cars and an ambulance with flashing lights parked in front of my building.

"Leatrice!" I grabbed Richard's arm and pulled him forward.

"That nutty old lady who's always trying to set you up with the UPS man?"

"Something must have happened to her." My mouth went dry. "She's old, Richard."

"She never seemed that old to me," Richard muttered as we ran up to the building. I went to knock on Leatrice's door on the first floor but heard loud voices and crackling radios coming from upstairs. I took the stairs two at a time and could hear Richard puffing behind me, the contents of his milk crate clattering as he tried to keep up. When we reached the fourth floor, I saw that my apartment door stood wide open and two uniformed police officers were in the hallway.

"What the hell is going on here?" I could feel the panic in my voice.

"I'm dying." Richard reached the top of the stairs and let the milk crate crash to the floor.

Leatrice rushed out from my apartment and threw her arms around me. "Thank heavens you're home."

"Leatrice." I pulled her away from me and tried to ignore the fact that she had loosely belted a brown raincoat over what had to be children's pajamas, complete with feet. "What are you doing in my apartment? What are the police doing here?"

"What is she wearing?" Richard looked up from where he leaned against one of the officers.

Detective Reese stepped out of my apartment. "Ms. Archer." He placed a hand on my shoulder. "I'm afraid you've been robbed."

Chapter 7

"Ransacked is more like it." Leatrice pulled me by the arm into my apartment. Papers were scattered all over the floor and my couch cushions had been tossed against the wall. The shopping bag full of clothes I'd meant to take to the dry cleaners the week before had been ripped open, its contents emptied onto a chair. Tiny candy hearts littered the floor in bits and pieces.

Detective Reese walked past me into the room. "From the looks of things, they didn't burglarize you."

"What were they doing then, redecorating?" Richard came in to stand next to me and had his hands on his hips surveying the damage.

"What I mean is that it appears that your stereo and TV were untouched. You'll have to check and see if the intruders took any jewelry, of course."

"I don't have any expensive jewelry."

"Now there's the real crime." Richard began picking my clothes up off the floor, and then spotted my dining table covered with scattered papers. "Look at the mess over here."

I glared at him. "Actually, the burglars didn't touch the table."

"Sorry," Richard mouthed.

"There's always a chance that the intruders were disturbed before they could take what they were after." Detective Reese leaned against the back of my couch. "Your neighbor made quite a racket."

I peered down at the tiny woman standing beside me. "Leatrice disturbed the burglars?"

"Well, I knew you weren't home." Leatrice patted my hand. "I saw you tear out of here earlier."

"An emergency?" Reese eyed the milk crate of cooking equipment that Richard had pushed into a corner.

"Something like that." I avoided the detective's eyes and turned my attention back to Leatrice.

"So when I heard someone throwing things around in your apartment, I knew it couldn't be you." Leatrice turned to smile at Reese. "She's such a nice girl. No parties or late-night guests like other young people have these days."

I heard Richard stifle a laugh, but I refused to look at him.

"Miss Archer is lucky to have such an observant neighbor." Reese returned Leatrice's smile. He probably loved this.

"Leatrice." I took a long breath. "How did you hear someone throwing cushions and clothes from four flights down?"

"Well, I came up to see if you were back home yet." Color began to creep up her neck and seep through the bright coral dabs of rouge applied to her cheeks. "I stood outside your door getting ready to knock when I heard the intruders."

"The truth comes out." Richard picked up a couch cushion and brushed the dust off, sending him into a coughing fit.

"Why are there so many cops here?" I asked Reese. "And why an ambulance?"

"Mrs. Butters requested every emergency vehicle in the city." Reese wasn't smiling.

Richard sat up from where he'd collapsed on the couch after his coughing fit. "Some people are so dramatic."

"Just trying to be helpful." Leatrice lowered her eyes to the floor. "I thought you were in trouble, dear."

Reese patted Leatrice on the arm. "Who knows what would have been taken if she hadn't called the police and set off her safety horn."

Richard lifted the arm he'd draped across his eyes. "Safety horn?"

"Half the neighborhood heard it." Leatrice beamed at me and produced the small red horn from her coat pocket. "Do you want me to show you how it works?"

Richard jumped up from the couch. "I'd like to see."

"No," I snapped. Richard made a face at me and sat back down.

"So what's the next step, Detective?" Leatrice reluctantly put the horn back in her pocket. "Should I come downtown with you?"

"We appreciate all your help, Mrs. Butters, but we've done about all we can do for now."

Leatrice cleared her throat. "But how are you going to find out who did it?"

"To be honest with you, we might not."

"What?" Leatrice and I spoke at the same time.

"We dusted for prints, but it appears the doorknobs were wiped clean or the intruder wore gloves." Reese slid his notebook into his blazer pocket.

"I hope your men are going to be cleaning up their dusting powder." Richard pulled a monogrammed handkerchief out of his jacket and waved it in front of his mouth. "One thing this apartment doesn't need is more dust."

"Or another smart comment," I said under my breath.

"Well, I'm just being honest, darling," he mumbled through the white linen.

Reese raised his voice. "I'm afraid without an eyewitness identification, we just don't have much to go on."

"You didn't see them leave?" I asked Leatrice. "I

thought you were standing by the front door."

"They left through the back door and down the fire escape," Reese answered for Leatrice. "Probably the point of entry, too."

"I've been meaning to get a new lock on that door for a while," I sighed. "It's loose."

"Do you think they'll come back and try again?" Richard's eyes darted to the back of the apartment.

"I'm sure these are just petty criminals." Reese started for the door. "I'd recommend changing your locks to be on the safe side, but otherwise you don't have to worry too much about them returning. I'll bet Mrs. Butters scared them pretty bad."

Richard followed after the detective. "Are you sure this isn't connected to Mrs. Pierce's death?"

Reese shook his head. "Doubtful."

"So it's just a coincidence that Annabelle finds a body and gets robbed all in the span of two days?" Richard's eyebrows popped up so high they almost disappeared under his choppy bangs.

"I'd say so." Reese stepped into the hall and the rest of the police officers followed him out. "Feel free to call me if anything else unusual happens, though."

"First a dead body, then a burglary," Richard said over his shoulder to me, but loud enough so Reese could hear. "I forget what comes next. Swarms of locusts or water into blood?"

Leatrice followed fast on the detective's heels and tried to talk over Richard. "So nice of you to come down personally, Detective."

Richard closed the door behind her and started pushing a bookshelf in front of the door.

"What are you doing?" I sat down on the sofa and kicked off my shoes. "The back door is the one they broke into."

Richard took off his suit jacket and pushed up the powder pink sleeves of his shirt.

"I'm not protecting us from the burglars," Richard said and gave me a disdainful look, "I'm saving us from Leatrice."

Chapter 8

"So we're all secured." Richard swung the milk crate onto the kitchen counter. "I pushed a table in front of the back door and made a pyramid of those little silver bells on top. If anyone tries to get in tonight, we'll hear them for sure."

My mouth fell open in surprise. "You used the silver-plated bells for Saturday's wedding as a booby trap?"

"Relax. They're not breakable." Richard bumped into me as he opened a cabinet. Definitely a kitchen designed for one. "The pyramid is fabulous. I think you should arrange them that way for the wedding."

"How many did you use?"

"All of them."

I felt a huge headache coming on. "Are you telling me that at this moment two hundred bells are stacked up against my back door?"

"You don't sound grateful, Annabelle." Richard pawed through the contents of the plastic crate and produced an aluminum tray covered in cling wrap.

I pressed my hands to my cheeks and tried to look sincere. "Oh, I'm sorry."

"Don't mention it, darling."

Richard missed my sarcasm.

"I wouldn't have dreamed of letting you stay here by yourself after what happened." Richard patted my arm.

Great, now I felt guilty. "I told you that I'd be fine."

"Just because you're an independent business woman doesn't mean you have to do everything on your own."

"I know. I'm just used to it." I squeezed his hand. "Thanks for staying with me."

Richard batted his eyelashes at me. "I only hope Leatrice doesn't consider it inappropriate that you're having a man stay over."

I groaned. "She's like a chaperone and a matchmaker all rolled into one."

"I must admit that I'm enjoying watching her try to set you up with our detective friend."

"Don't you dare encourage her." I wagged a finger in his face.

"Encourage her?" Richard unwrapped the foil tray and tossed the wadded-up plastic wrap in the metal trash can in the corner. "She doesn't need any encouragement."

"That's the problem." I rubbed my temples.

"This will make you feel better." Richard began

unloading the contents of the disposable tray onto a plate. "I saved some hors d'oeuvres from the party."

"Good. I'm starving." I watched Richard arrange a handful of crab puffs and Brie tartlets on a dinner plate and place it in the microwave. "Someone didn't let me eat anything all night."

"You're breaking my heart, Annabelle." Richard opened my refrigerator. "There's not a drop to drink in this house, is there?"

"Not unless you want coffee."

Richard closed the door with his hip. "That would calm my nerves and help me sleep better."

"I might have some decaf."

"Never mind. I think I have a bottle of leftover champagne." Richard emptied the rest of the milk crate and held up a bottle with a white label and heavy gold lettering. He made a face. "It's warm."

"That's okay. I've got ice."

"Normally I'd be horrified." Richard peeled off the foil and popped the cork into a yellow-striped dishtowel. "But desperate times call for desperate measures."

I pulled two fat mugs down from the cabinet and filled them with ice.

Richard eyed the mugs. "You must be joking. This is champagne, Annabelle, not Ovaltine."

"Sorry. I don't have much occasion to use fancy champagne flutes."

"Pity." Richard poured the champagne into the mugs and took them into the living room. I followed him

63

with the microwaved plate of hors d'oeuvres, holding it by the edges with paper napkins so I wouldn't burn my fingers.

"You can put it here." Richard motioned to a space he'd cleared on the coffee table. He pulled one of the paper napkins from under the plate. "Who are Martha and Matt?"

"One of my couples who got married last year." I grabbed a cushion from the couch.

"And why do you have their cocktail napkins?" Richard held up a white napkin with shiny silver script.

"I called the clients for months but they never picked them up." I shrugged my shoulders. "One day I needed a napkin, so I started using them."

Richard dabbed his mouth with the napkin. "Remind me not to leave anything behind."

"Let's see how good these famous Brie tartlets are when they're reheated." I took a bite of one and the crispy sugar topping crackled in my mouth. "Not bad. Kind of like a pungent crème brûlée."

"Be careful." Richard scowled as I dribbled some of the hot Brie onto the couch.

"It's okay." I dismissed his concern and scraped at the small spot of Brie with my finger. "This cotton twill is easy to clean."

"That's all well and good, but you're not the one who has to sleep on it."

"Richard, I said you can take the bed and I'll take the couch." I took a drink of watery champagne to cool my mouth from the hot cheese. "I know how your neck gets if you don't sleep on a proper mattress."

Richard nibbled on the edge of a crab puff. "I wouldn't hear of it. Besides, I should be near the front door in case the burglars come back."

"They broke in the back door, remember? The door near my bedroom."

"Which is all the more reason they'd try a different door." Richard's eyes disappeared behind his mug as he took a drink. "To surprise us."

"Very funny," I gave Richard a saccharine smile, then got serious. "You don't think they'll try to break in again, do you?"

"No," Richard assured me. "I think we're safe for now."

I snatched the last crab puff off the plate. "What do you mean, for now? You don't agree with Detective Reese that it was a random break-in?"

"It seems too coincidental to me." Richard pulled his legs up onto the couch and folded them Indian-style. "How many times have you found a dead body? Once. How many times has your apartment been broken into? Once."

"Okay, so it's a bit odd that they both happened within a couple of days. I'll give you that."

"And why did the burglar take nothing?"

"I think Leatrice did a pretty thorough job of scaring the burglars off before they were able to get anything." I finished the last of my champagne and stood up, stacking my mug on top of the empty plate. I continued talking as I headed for the kitchen. "I'm thinking of

65

buying a safety horn myself."

"Maybe she scared the burglars away, but why did they bother to throw things around? Not that you can tell the difference."

"Hey! I heard that." I refilled my mug with champagne and brought the bottle with me to the living room. "So what's your theory, then?"

Richard held out his mug for me to fill. "I think they were after something."

"If they didn't want valuables, then what could I have that any thief would want?"

"Good question." Richard let out a deep breath as he scanned my apartment. "Maybe this particular thief obsessively collects scrap paper and old magazines."

"Have I told you how hilarious you are?" I arched a brow at Richard.

He blew me a kiss, and then sat up straight. "If we're going with the theory that the murder and the break-in are connected, then they had to be searching for something to do with the Pierce wedding."

"Let me see if the file is gone. I left it on the table earlier today." I went to the dining table and began sifting through the mess of papers. I held up a purple accordion folder. "Here it is."

Richard hopped up and craned his neck over my shoulder as I flipped through the papers inside the file. "Is there anything missing?"

"I don't think so. Except for the guest list that Reese took with him."

"Maybe that's what they were after." Richard began

66

pacing up and down the length of the room. He stopped at my large front window and began fussing with the curtain ties. "Someone could look right in here if you're not careful."

"I don't think they could see much. We're on the fourth floor, after all."

"You never know. People are so nosy these days." Richard pulled the curtains together tightly, and then peeked back out through a tiny gap. "Why, I can see right into the house across the street from here."

"They always keep their curtains open."

"Do you ever see anything good happen?" Richard pulled his head out of the crack in the curtains and glanced over his shoulder at me.

I shook a finger at him, and he stepped away from the window, mumbling something I couldn't quite hear. Knowing Richard, I wasn't sorry I missed the comment.

I tossed the Pierce file on the table and sank back onto the couch. "Maybe we're going about this all the wrong way. What if Mrs. Pierce's ghost came back to haunt me and ransacked the place?"

"It would be just like her to be high-maintenance even when she's dead."

"Putting the poltergeist idea aside, is the missing guest list our only motive? That wasn't a big secret, so why go to all the trouble to break into my apartment for it?"

"I don't know what they were after, but since nothing is missing, I think we can assume that they didn't find it. And if it has something to do with Mrs. Pierce's death, you can believe they'll be back."

"What are we going to do?" I felt a little light-headed and doubted that the champagne had anything to do with it. Even if we had finished the bottle.

"We'll just have to figure out who's behind this little break-in before they can try again." Richard sounded more confident than I felt.

I swallowed hard and felt my mouth go dry. "If the killer and the burglar are the same person, we have to find them before they *kill* again."

Chapter 9

"Do you really think Mrs. Pierce's death and the break-in are connected?" Kate handed me a white paper bag as I got in her car. "Your favorite chocolate croissants from Patisserie Poupon."

Chocolate for breakfast. I'd have to start my diet the next day.

"Remind me to give you a raise." I pulled a croissant out of the bag and a shower of buttery flakes fell onto my lap.

"I figure you deserve indulging after what happened last night." Kate jerked the car into traffic, and I heard the cacophony of car horns that usually accompanied her driving. "Weren't you frightened to stay at your apartment after someone broke in?"

"With Richard to protect me? Why would I be afraid?"

Kate laughed. "If I were you, I'd want to spend the whole day in bed recovering from the shock." Kate gave me a sideways glance as she swerved around a van double-parked in the street. "Do you mind if I ask what those marks on the side of your face are?"

I pulled down the window visor and examined myself in the tiny mirror. "Oh, great. I've got marks from the sisal area rug. I got ready so fast I didn't even check myself in the mirror."

"You slept on the floor?"

"Not on purpose." I flipped the visor back up. "We ended up staying awake pretty late and just fell asleep in the living room with all the lights on."

"The illustrious Richard Gerard sleeping on the floor? Now that's a sight I'd love to see."

"Well, you missed your big chance." I folded up the empty bag and tucked it in the glove compartment. "He's off to the Phillips Collection to see if Mrs. Pierce had any connection there, then to the police station to try to clear his name."

Kate sighed. "I wish we had a reason to stop by the police station and see all those cute cops again."

"Sorry to deprive you, but we have to pay condolences and see if we turn up any clues."

"After our cake appointment with Meredith Murphy, right?"

I slapped my hand to my forehead. "I almost forgot we had a meeting this morning. Good thing you reminded me."

"I'm sure Meredith's mother would have understood

if we missed the meeting. She's so easygoing." Kate winked at me and we both burst into laughter. Meredith Murphy's mother had a facial twitch that I attributed to her being as high-strung as a Chihuahua. Kate insisted it must be a result of multiple facelifts.

We burned a yellow light as we turned onto a residential street behind the Georgetown cemetery. Kate rolled through a stop sign and angled her car into a space on the street. I hopped out of the car and scanned the fronts of the nearly identical row houses until I found the one with the Christmas lights still wrapped around the top of the porch. Our favorite cake baker, Alexandra, had her cake studio in the basement of her fashionable Upper Georgetown house.

"With five minutes to spare," Kate sounded out of breath as we climbed the stone stairs to the house.

I leaned on the doorbell, then brushed the last croissant crumbs off my skirt. "Are the marks on my face gone?"

She glanced at me. "Pretty much."

The front door opened and Alexandra waved us in. I'd always thought that bakers should be round, jolly people, but Alexandra had changed my preconceived idea. Thin and sophisticated, she spoke with a slight accent that I could place vaguely in Eastern Europe. She never claimed any one country. *Just a little bit of everywhere,* she said.

Today Alexandra had thrown her long brown hair into a loose bun fastened with chopsticks and wore a body-hugging turquoise dress with matching strappy sandals. Her talent for making clothes look perfect came second only to her ability to create stunning wedding cakes. If she weren't so nice, I'd hate her.

She motioned downstairs and rolled her eyes. "They arrived early."

"How's it going?" Kate whispered.

Alexandra picked up a glass of wine from the entryway table. "Do you want some?"

"That bad, huh?" I groaned.

"Well, they got better after my first glass." She nudged me and giggled. "Come see for yourself."

We followed her down the narrow staircase to the studio. Shelves lining the back wall of the room displayed sample cakes decorated in elaborate sugar flowers and swags of edible ribbon. A whitewashed wooden table dominated most of the room and held stacks of photo albums.

Meredith Murphy and her mother were sitting at the table flipping through pictures of wedding cakes. You'd never guess that the mother had the highlighted ponytail and too-tight top and the daughter wore a mousy brown bob and linen blazer. I always felt as if I'd stepped into a real-life *Freaky Friday* when I saw the two together.

Mrs. Murphy glanced up at us as we sat down across from them. "I'm glad you're here. Which is fancier, Annabelle, buttercream icing or fondant?"

I tried not to cringe as I imagined Mrs. Murphy's concept of fancy. I should consider myself lucky that she didn't want a Chippendale's dancer jumping out of the cake.

"For your July wedding, I'd go with fondant. Since it has an elastic texture, as opposed to the softness of the buttercream, fondant will hold up to the heat much better."

Mrs. Murphy nodded. "We like the big bows on the top with the ribbons coming down the sides." She held up a laminated photo of a five-tiered cake dominated by a cascade of bows and ribbons.

"I like the cakes with just a few sugar roses, Mother." The bride's voice hardly rose above a whisper.

"Don't be silly, Meredith," her mother snapped. "The bow on the cake will match the bow on your invitation."

"We haven't made a final decision on invitations yet, and I don't like the one with the bow."

This could get ugly. I'd seen fistfights break out over bows before. "Perhaps you could select two different cake designs and wait until later to decide which one fits the design of the wedding."

"I'd be happy to sketch out two options for you," Alexandra said. Her expression said she would do anything to get them out of there. A glass of wine was starting to sound good.

"Thank you." The bride's voice sounded louder, and she almost smiled.

"Whatever you want, Meredith." Her mother pressed her lips together and tossed her ponytail off her shoulder. "After all, it is your wedding."

Kate kicked me under the table. We always said that if we had a dollar for every time we heard that phrase, we'd be millionaires. If we had a dollar for each time it was sincere, we'd barely be able to split a latte.

We followed the bride and her mother up the stairs and said good-bye to them at the door so we could debrief with Alexandra. I marveled at how the mother could walk down the steep stairs to the sidewalk in her high-heeled mules. I'd never seen the woman wearing age-appropriate clothing and shuddered to think of her interpretation of a proper mother-of-the-bride dress. I hoped there wasn't a line of eveningwear tube tops.

Kate let out a long breath after the door closed. "What is it with these mothers?"

"They aren't all bad, Kate. Remember the one last year who baked us cookies?"

Kate counted off a finger. "That's one."

"I heard you got rid of our worst one the other night." Alexandra crossed her arms over her chest. "Don't forget I had to do four tastings for Mrs. Pierce to make sure the crème brûlée filling for her cake had enough crackle for her."

In all the chaos, it had slipped my mind that Alexandra had done the wedding cake for the Pierce wedding. By the time we found the body, the cake had been set up for hours and she had been long gone.

"You make it sound like we killed her," I said.

Alexandra winked. "I just wish I could have helped whoever did."

I shuddered. "Don't joke about it. I think we're still

on the suspect list. I know Richard is."

Alexandra's mouth fell open. "They think he had something to do with the death?" She knew Richard well since she created the cakes for almost all his parties. "Have they met Richard?"

"The only reason he's a suspect is because of the poison," I explained.

Alexandra shook her head. "Richard would never ruin his food, even to murder someone he despised."

"Did the police question you?" Kate sounded hesitant. "After all, you did bake the wedding cake."

Alexandra's face lit up. "Actually a cute detective came by yesterday. Since my cake wasn't cut or served, he said questioning me was just a formality."

"That must have been a short interview." I couldn't help hoping that Reese hadn't spent long with the city's sexiest baker.

"I did tell him about the fight I witnessed between Mr. and Mrs. Pierce."

I exchanged a look with Kate. "When did you see them fighting?"

Alexandra paused as if trying to remember. "I left the museum as the bridal party arrived to take photos. I remember seeing the Pierces in the entrance foyer as I went out the front door. I couldn't hear what they were saying, but they were definitely arguing."

"Did the detective seem interested in what you saw?" Kate asked.

Alexandra shrugged. "He didn't seem too surprised. I guess investigating all of Mrs. Pierce's fights is a big job. He seemed to be pretty focused on the food angle. Bad luck for Richard, I'm afraid."

"I'm sure he'll be cleared soon," I said with more confidence than I felt. "He planned to go talk to someone this morning."

Alexandra gave us a mischievous grin. "Tell him if he ends up in jail, I'll bake him a cake with a nail file in it."

"I don't think that would do any good," I sighed. "Knowing Richard, he'd just give himself a pedicure."

"I want to hear more about the wedding and the murder." Alexandra looked positively giddy. "Can you stay for lunch?"

"I wish we could." Boy, I meant it. Alexandra could cook as expertly as she baked, and my stomach growled at the thought of her curried chicken salad. "We have a full day of appointments."

"I should get to work on those two sketches, anyway." Alexandra gave us air kisses. "I promise to make the drawing of the cake with bows hideous."

I smiled all the way to the car imagining Mrs. Murphy's face when she got the sketches.

"Are you sure you still want to go 'pay condolences'?" Kate made air quotes with her fingers.

"It's the least we can do, Kate. Who knows what we'll find out?"

"I think this is an exercise in fertility, but okay."

I shook my head as I stepped into the car. "Just drive."

Chapter 10

"I still don't understand why we're offering condolences for a person we couldn't stand." Kate sounded exasperated as she drummed her fingers on the steering wheel. If she saw me glaring at her, she pretended not to notice.

"Because it's the polite thing to do, Kate. Anyway, we've got a good reason. Self-preservation."

"Hey, it's not me they're after." She paused behind a line of cars waiting to turn left.

"If I get killed, you're out of a job, remember?"

"Good point. But explain to me again how this is going to help us find the killer."

"I'm willing to bet that one of her husbands killed her. Either Dr. Pierce or her ex-husband, Dr. Harriman. You heard what Alexandra said about Dr. Pierce." I motioned for Kate to turn before we reached Dupont Circle. "So I figure we should hang around people who know them and keep our ears open."

"But we're going to the bride's house first." Kate sounded confused. "You think she had something to do with it?"

"We're just acting concerned. I don't think Elizabeth could disagree with her mother, much less kill her."

Kate shook her head. "You know what they say about the nice, quiet ones?"

"Not this quiet one. Park anywhere in the next three

blocks. Her house is right behind embassy row."

Kate backed into a parking space and ran one tire up onto the curb. "Maybe she got fed up with her mother controlling her life and flipped out."

"And ruined her own wedding?"

"You're right. Murdering her mother is plausible, but ruining her own wedding is inconceivable." Kate stepped out of the car and smoothed down her black wrap dress. "Which house is hers?"

I looked down at the address on the slip of paper and pointed to a red brick townhouse a few doors down. Mrs. Pierce had run the entire wedding operation out of her home in Chevy Chase and I could drive there in my sleep, but I'd never been to the bride's house before.

"Do you think you could have picked a less somber dress, Kate?" I eyed her clingy dress with a plunging front.

"What are you talking about? It has long sleeves and it's black."

"I'm talking about the neckline. Doesn't exactly scream 'mourning,' does it?" I'd chosen a black crepe suit that buttoned to my collarbone and had a knee-length skirt. I felt like a nun next to Kate.

"I think it's a good compromise." Kate walked up to the front door and pressed on the bell.

"What kind of a compromise?"

"I'm sad that I found a dead body, but I'm not all that sad that it was Clara Pierce." Kate pulled the front of the dress closed a fraction. "It also transitions from day to evening beautifully."

The front door opened, and Dr. Andrew Donovan stood in the doorway wearing wrinkled chinos and an untucked green Polo shirt. He looked nothing like the dashing groom from the wedding night. I stepped forward and took his hand.

"Annabelle and Kate from Wedding Belles. Your wedding planners." I hurried my prepared speech. "We just wanted to stop by and check on Elizabeth. How is she?"

"Of course, I remember you." Dr. Donovan stepped back into the house and opened the door. "Please come in."

I pushed Kate inside and closed the door behind me. "We don't want to intrude. We're just so worried about her."

"We grow so attached to our brides." Kate had such a serious expression on her face that I had to avert my eyes to keep from laughing. Kate didn't grow attached to anyone who didn't have an Adam's apple.

"It's kind of you to come." The groom showed us into the den. I perched on the edge of a wingback chair, and Kate sat on the burgundy leather couch. "I'm afraid Elizabeth isn't handling her mother's death well. You saw how she went to pieces at the wedding."

"Is she at home?"

"We've had to sedate her." Dr. Donovan shook his head. "She's not in any condition to see visitors."

I tried to sound solemn. "Of course not."

"We spoke to the police, of course." The doctor

picked at a loose thread on the hem of his shirt. "But there's not much we can tell them. Did the police question you?"

"Yes, but we don't know anything, either," Kate said. "Aside from finding the body."

"In all the drama, I'd forgotten that you two found my mother-in-law. That must have been quite a shock."

"You can say that again." Kate shuddered, and I shot her a look. Before I could try to smooth over Kate's blunder, my cell phone began ringing to the tune of "Here Comes the Bride." I fumbled in my bag to find it.

The groom stood and managed a weak smile. "Do you mind if I go check on Elizabeth for a moment? I don't like to leave her alone for too long." Dr. Donovan backed out of the room.

I retrieved my phone, and Kate stuck a finger down her throat. She hated my personalized ring.

"Wedding Belles, this is Annabelle."

"Hi, Annabelle. It's Kimberly Kinkaid." The bride for this Saturday. I always gave brides my cell phone number the week of the wedding and not a moment sooner.

"Hi, Kimberly. Is everything okay?"

"Well, I know this number is for important calls, but I need your help with something." Her voice sounded even more tentative than usual.

I braced myself for a bridal breakdown. "That's what I'm here for."

"I've been thinking about the rose petals outside during the ceremony."

"The ones that the florist is going to scatter down the aisle?"

"Right," she barreled on. "What if the wind blows?"

"What do you mean?" I tried not to sound impatient.

"I don't want them blowing out of the aisle. I want them in a straight line."

"Well, there's not much we can do if the wind blows them around, Kimberly."

"Can you pin them down to the ground?"

Was she serious? "You want me to pin the rose petals in place?" I heard Kate stifle a laugh, but I couldn't look at her for fear I would burst into laughter.

"Or maybe there's a special adhesive to glue them to the grass?" It was official. She had lost her mind.

I needed to get off the phone before Dr. Donovan came back and heard me debating ways to adhere flower petals to grass. I kept my voice steady, despite Kate's muffled cackling behind me. "Why don't I check on that special adhesive and give you a call back?"

I flipped my phone off and dropped it in my bag. "Nice, Kate. We're paying condolences and you're laughing your head off."

"I couldn't help it." Kate stood up and walked around the room. "I'm sure Dr. Donovan didn't hear me and even if he did, I'll bet he wouldn't care."

My jaw dropped. "You don't think he'd care that you're laughing while his new bride is practically in a coma?"

"I just mean that he has so much on his mind that he wouldn't notice. I didn't catch him peeking down my dress once."

"I wasn't aware that cleavage is a test of how distraught someone is."

Kate faced the wall, studying a row of framed diplomas. "It's one of them."

I held up a hand. "Spare me the others."

"Check out this guy's credentials." Kate whistled. "No wonder Mrs. Pierce adored him so much. Princeton undergrad. Harvard Med."

I walked up next to Kate. "She wouldn't have accepted anything less. Both her husbands went to Ivy League schools, too."

"Talk about being label-conscious. At least he seems like a nice guy."

"Yeah. With all these fancy diplomas, you'd think he'd be a pompous jerk."

"He's a bit dull for my taste, but nice enough, I suppose. It's true when people say you can't judge a book by what it covers."

I think she enjoyed watching me cringe. "Close enough."

"Let's get out of here, Annie. This visit has been a total waste, if we're supposed to be looking for clues." Kate tugged her dress together in the front. "What's our next stop?"

"Mrs. Pierce's house. It should be the perfect opportunity to talk to Dr. Pierce."

"So after that all we have to worry about is finding

the ex-husband?"

"Right." I sat back down and leaned my head against the chair. "Dr. Harriman. I remember him from the ceremony, but only vaguely."

"I might be able to assist you in that regard." Just then, a tall man with dark, silvering hair stepped into the room. "I'm Dr. Harriman."

Chapter 11

"Now that you've found me, how can I be of service?" Dr. Harriman took a few long strides into the room and sat down in the bottle-green armchair across from me. "Are you friends of Elizabeth?"

I let myself breathe again, and I could see Kate relax as she sat down next to me. He must not have overheard much of our conversation.

"Actually, Dr. Harriman, we're your daughter's wedding planners." I managed a smile in his direction. "We wanted to offer our condolences to the family."

"That's thoughtful of you." He pulled a cigar out of the pocket of his tweed jacket and rolled it back and forth between his thumb and index finger. "My ex-wife's death has been a terrible shock to us all."

"I can only imagine, sir." I shook my head along with him. Right. He probably couldn't wait for us to leave so he could light up his cigar and celebrate.

Dr. Harriman pocketed the cigar again. "Of course it's hardest on Elizabeth. She's been hysterical since they found Clara at the reception. I came over to be here with her and help her cope with the tragedy."

"Of course." I pulled my skirt down over my knees. I hoped Kate would get my hint and do the same thing. "Unfortunately, we're the people who found Mrs. Pierce."

He shifted his eyes from me to Kate. "Yes. I remember seeing you with the police."

"You were one of the doctors called to the scene of the crime, right?" Kate's eyes darted to me. Surprising that she remembered anyone being around except the cute police officers.

Dr. Harriman looked at his hands and nodded. "I couldn't help her, though. She was dead by the time she hit the floor."

"So the fall caused her death, then?" I tried to make my question sound casual.

He glanced up at me. "What else could it have been?"

Kate gave a loud, hacking cough, and Dr. Harriman stood up to hand her his handkerchief. Kate's dress gaped open as she reached forward, and I motioned for her to close it as the doctor turned to sit back down. She ignored me.

"We've taken up enough of your time, Dr. Harriman." I stood up and Kate followed, handing the handkerchief back unused. "Please give our condolences to Elizabeth."

"I'll be sure to tell her you stopped by when she wakes up." He led us to the foyer and shook our hands, then closed the door behind us.

"Don't say anything until we get in the car." I spoke with a grin fixed on my face, in case anyone watching us could read lips.

"I don't think he can hear us." Kate crossed the street and unlocked the car. I waited until we got inside and closed the doors.

"Okay, now we can talk." I fastened my seat belt snugly as Kate rolled the car off the curb. We tapped the bumper of the SUV in front of us. "What do you think of our suspect being the examining doctor?"

"I think you almost blew it. We're not supposed to know that she may have been poisoned, remember?"

"I know. But why do you think he didn't mention the rash or the possibility that the fall wasn't what killed her?"

"Because he's not supposed to discuss it with anyone, I'd imagine."

"I guess you're right." I put my sunglasses on top of my head to hold back my hair. "Unless he wanted to play down the poisoning angle because he's the one who poisoned her."

Kate weaved her way through traffic as we headed toward Chevy Chase. "I'll play along. Let's say he poisoned her. How did he do it?"

I threw out a guess. "Maybe he injected her at the crime scene and pretended to be trying to save her life."

"Why poison her when, at least as far as we could tell, she was already dead? Anyway, how could he have pulled out a needle with all those cops around, not to mention the other doctors?"

"Okay, so he injected her earlier in the night." I pressed my foot instinctively against the floor of the car as we approached a yellow light.

"So he just goes up to his ex-wife, jabs her with a needle, and they both go along their merry little ways?" Kate sped up and we burned the red light. "That doesn't sound like the Clara Pierce I knew and loathed."

"So the theory has a few holes." I looked out my window as we passed the National Cathedral. Tour buses were lined up three deep in front, and Kate honked as one tried to merge in front of us. Kate hated when cars tried to get in front of her.

"Listen, Annabelle, I can tell you that Dr. Harriman wasn't as upset as his son-in-law."

"What do you mean? The cleavage test?"

Kate nodded. "He peeked."

"Well for God's sake, Kate, you have to make an effort not to look. I don't even know if I passed your cleavage test."

"I'm guessing that he didn't like his ex-wife, but Dr. Harriman doesn't seem like a sinister murderer to me."

I recognized that tone of voice. "You think he's attractive, don't you?" My mouth fell open as I watched Kate begin to blush. "I can't believe it. You've got a crush on one of our suspects."

"I do not." Kate's voice cracked. "I just think he's polite and distinguished."

"God help me. I've got Mata Hari as a sidekick."

My cell phone began singing, and I retrieved it from the side pocket of my purse. Richard's number popped up on the display and I flipped it open.

"Tell me you're having better luck than we are, Richard."

"Didn't you get my message?" He sounded exasperated. "I spent half the morning at the Phillips Collection and didn't get anywhere with that dreadful woman in charge of events. I'm almost grateful she took me off her list of approved caterers."

"So you couldn't find any connection to Mrs. Pierce?"

"Not a thing," Richard said over a lot of background noise. He must have been at the police station. "How's your detective work going?"

"Not bad if Kate would stop eliminating suspects because they're too attractive to be murderers."

"Too bad we don't have any solid female leads," Richard responded. "At least that would cut down on the chances of her dating the killer."

"What's he saying about me?" Kate grabbed for the phone.

"Just that he finds it highly unlikely you'd base a decision on physical attributes alone," I said with a straight face.

"Of course she wouldn't use just physical qualities, Annabelle. Don't forget money. That's at least number two on her list."

I tried not to break into a grin. "You're right, Richard."

"What's he saying now?" Kate sounded suspicious.

"That I was off-base when I implied you judge people by only one criterion."

"Good," Kate threw her chin out. "Tell Richard I'm sorry I assumed he was teasing me."

I tried to keep a straight face. "Did you hear that, Richard?"

"Each delicious word of it."

"Yes, I know you're sorry about all the times you teased Kate."

"Hey, that's not what I said," Richard protested.

"It's about time he apologized for all the cracks he makes about my social life," Kate insisted.

"He feels awful." I mouthed the words to Kate while I listened to Richard's complaints getting louder in my ear.

"That's fine, Annabelle." Richard sighed deeply. "Mock me. Make light of your dear friend who's stuck in this godforsaken police department with nothing to drink but vending-machine coffee."

"I'm not mocking you." Fabulous. He'd become a martyr in the span of two hours.

"I think the police are looking at me funny, too."

"Why?" I asked. "What are you wearing?"

"Nothing flashy. Just my silver paisley jacket with matching flat-front pants."

Just what I would have chosen for a visit to the police station.

"I'm sure when they finally give me back my equipment and let me reopen my business there'll be a few jobs for me." Richard sucked in his breath. "Perhaps I can specialize in catering for pet funerals."

"Don't be ridiculous." I grabbed the dashboard as Kate made a sharp left into a residential neighborhood.

"You think I'm overreacting to being a prime suspect in a murder case? I feel light-headed, Annabelle. My whole career is flashing before my eyes."

"Put your head between your knees."

"I can't. These pants are too tight."

"Can you lie down?"

"Have you ever seen the floor at a police station?" Richard's voice rose an octave.

"Why don't you go to the bathroom and splash your face with water?" I closed my eyes so I wouldn't have to see Kate roll through one stop sign after another.

"The bathroom is even worse than the floor. I'm not setting foot in there without a can of scrubbing bubbles and a pair of rubber gloves."

"I've got to go, Richard." I opened my eyes as the car slowed down, then jerked to a stop. "We're at Mrs. Pierce's house."

"Okay, I'm going to go see if I have some handi-wipes in my car." With the prospect of something to fuss over, Richard already sounded better. "Call me later."

I dropped the phone in my purse and let out a long breath.

"I take it things with the police aren't going well." Kate parked the car across from the Pierce home, with the passenger side halfway in a ditch. The massive stone house already had cars lined up bumper-to-bumper in its circular driveway.

"You know Richard. When is he ever not on his deathbed?" I opened my car door and almost rolled out onto the grass.

"I hope this doesn't take too long. I need to find a site for the Bailey wedding by tomorrow." Kate extended a leg out of the car and paused. "Do you hear music?"

"It sounds like a party." I nodded toward the house. "I think it's coming from inside."

We watched a woman in a short Pucci dress and stiletto heels step out of a convertible she'd parked in the middle of the street. A valet in a blue jacket appeared as if by magic and took her car keys from her. We followed from a distance as she walked to the marble-columned entrance of the house. The front door flew open and high-pitched laughter spilled out-side as the woman exchanged air kisses with someone and disappeared inside the house. My eyes widened.

"They've got valet?"

"Now this is more like it." Kate adjusted the neckline of her dress to display ample cleavage. "I knew I picked out the perfect dress this morning."

Chapter 12

I stood inside the expansive marble foyer of the Pierce home and tried to stop myself from gaping. "I can't believe I'm saying this, Kate. For once, you're dressed appropriately."

A woman wearing a tight suede pantsuit edged by us, followed by a tall redhead in a black halter dress cut down to her navel. Could anyone ever pass the cleavage test in that dress?

"Wakes sure have changed a lot." Kate stepped out of the way of one of the many waiters bustling around the house.

"Welcome, ladies." A statuesque blonde in a pink silk-shantung suit approached us, beaming from ear to ear. From her accent, I placed her firmly below the Mason-Dixon line. "I'm Bev Tripton. Clara's best friend in the whole wide world."

So this was the best friend.

"Annabelle and Kate." I extended my hand and she gave me the tips of her fingers to shake. "We worked with Mrs. Pierce on Elizabeth's wedding."

Bev grabbed me by the shoulders. "Wedding Belles, right? Precious name."

"We don't mean to interrupt anything." I noticed a string quartet playing in the corner. "We just stopped by to pay our condolences to Dr. Pierce."

"Well, that's just about the sweetest thing I've ever

heard." Bev pulled me forward by the elbow. "You must join us, girls. We're celebrating Clara's life. No sense in getting bogged down in sadness, right?"

"I guess not." I motioned for Kate to follow as Bev led me into the sunken living room. The house looked totally different from what I remembered. The pale peach couches had been removed and people sat at cocktail tables covered in red crushed velvet. A bar stood in the corner, and most of the men were gathered there. I spotted Dr. Pierce with a drink in one hand. He didn't seem distraught for a man whose wife had just died. The oversized green martini didn't help his case.

"Clara loved a good party, so I said to myself, 'Bev, what better way to honor her memory than to have a huge blowout?'"

"I won't forget it anytime soon," Kate said quietly enough so only I heard.

"Help yourself to the food stations." Bev stepped away, still smiling. "But don't spoil your appetite. The cherries jubilee display gets wheeled out in twenty minutes."

Kate linked her arm through mine. "So, what's our strategy? Should we hit the raw bar first or the risotto station?"

"We're not here to eat, Kate. We're supposed to be getting information."

"We just got some valuable information. Her friends hated her even more than we did."

"This is some party, isn't it?" I blinked twice as I spotted an ice sculpture of a mermaid rising like Venus out of the center of the raw bar. "Maybe Bev was being sincere and this really is a tribute to . . . Is that a contortionist?"

We craned our necks to see a leotard-clad performer hop through the room with one leg hooked around his neck.

"Did Bev rent the cast of Cirque du Soleil?" Kate took two glasses of champagne from a waiter and handed one to me. "She only sounds sincere because she's Southern. Believe me, this is no tribute."

"After overhearing those people at Richard's party, I knew a lot of people didn't like her," I said in shock. "But you'd think that at least her best friend and her husband would be a little more discreet with their feelings."

"Speaking of being more discreet." Kate nudged me hard and sloshed a bit of champagne on my sleeve. "Look over there."

I followed Kate's gaze and watched Bev nuzzle up to Dr. Pierce, then whisper something in his ear. He laughed and slipped an arm low around her waist.

"The husband and the best friend." I put my glass down on an end table. "So those women at the party were right."

Kate narrowed her eyes. "This isn't a new thing. They're way too comfortable with each other."

"Are you sure?"

Kate crossed her arms and stared at me.

"Okay, I forgot." I threw up my hands. "You're the expert."

"I wonder how long they've been having an affair under Clara's nose."

"This must be what the Pierces were fighting about. I find it hard to believe that Mrs. Pierce didn't put a stop to this."

"Unless she died before she got the chance." A look of panic crossed Kate's face. "Hurry, there's a mime heading our way."

"I can't move." I pointed to the wall of people blocking the path to the foyer. An opening began to appear. Too late. The mime materialized in front of us, and began furtive attempts to free himself from an imaginary box. I hated mimes. Kate elbowed her way through the crowd, and I followed close behind, escaping the silent performer still trapped in his box.

"Dr. Pierce had a pretty strong motive to kill his wife," Kate said as we made our way to the door.

"It could've been Bev. A rich doctor is a good catch for her."

"If Bev is twisted enough to throw a party like this when her best friend dies, she's twisted enough to commit murder," Kate said. "Where there's smoke, there's a liar."

I didn't correct her. In this case, it seemed to work.

"If we can find out more about the affair between Bev and Dr. Pierce, we'll be one step closer to figuring out who had motive enough to kill our client." I ducked as a stilt-walker stepped over me. "And I know exactly who can give us the dirt."

"Who?" Kate paused with one hand on the doorknob.

"Who's been doing the hair of every rich society lady for the past ten years, including Mrs. Pierce?"

"Why didn't I think of him first?" Kate exclaimed as she pulled open the front door. "I guess this means we aren't staying for the cherries jubilee?"

I rolled my eyes and gave Kate a push out the door. "Let's go talk to Fern."

Chapter 13

Fern stopped in midsnip as Kate and I walked into his Georgetown salon. "I don't believe my eyes."

He must have been finishing up the last client of the day because the salon was otherwise empty. The narrow shop always reminded me of a palace rather than a beauty parlor. Instead of the usual wall of mirrors, each of the three stylists had an ornate, gold mirror in front of his chair with a towering, carved wooden credenza to hold their supplies. This is what the "Cut and Curl" at Versailles must have looked like.

"Girls! I wondered how long you would go between appointments." He rushed over and embraced me, taking a handful of my hair and examining the split ends. He turned to hug Kate, and then pulled the top of her head to within an inch of his face. "I hope you don't tell people that I do your hair."

I smiled to the client, who tapped her watch. "Fern, we're not here about our hair. We just wanted to talk."

"Wait just a second." He returned to his client, analyzed her haircut from all angles, then pulled off her smock with a flourish and tipped her out of his chair. I watched in amazement. Fern's ability to stay pristine while cutting and coloring has always baffled me. I've never seen him with a single hair on him. As usual, he wore his own dark hair smoothed back, with not a strand out of place. The only flash of color in his all-black ensemble came from an enormous topaz ring on his right hand.

After the customer had left, Fern patted the seats of two shampoo chairs. "Okay, let's fix these disasters."

I brushed away a hair that had landed on my jacket. "Like I said, we're just here to catch up on our gossip."

"Besides, we don't have appointments," Kate said.

"We'll make a deal." Fern pulled two fluffy beige towels down from a shelf. "You let me fix your hair and save my reputation, and I'll tell you anything you want to know. After all the brides you've sent me, a little trim is nothing."

I looked at the clock on the wall. Five o'clock. Well, I didn't have any plans for the evening.

"Fine with me." I shrugged, taking the black smock he handed me and surrendering my suit jacket. "How about you, Kate?"

She lowered herself into a chair and winked at Fern. "As long as I can be out by seven. Hot date."

"When I'm done with you, your date won't be able to keep his hands off you." Fern gave Kate a knowing look and motioned for me to sit in the chair next to her.

Kate rubbed her hands together. "Work your magic."

"If you're good, I'll tell you a secret to drive your date wild." Fern winked. Getting some rather questionable advice on men came with all of Fern's haircuts.

"It's like gasoline to a flame." I groaned as I sat down and let Fern push my head back into a black basin. He stood between Kate and me, and turned on the water for both of us.

"Too hot?"

I shook my head as he wrapped a towel around my neck and began massaging my scalp with his fingers. "Did you hear what happened to Mrs. Pierce, Fern?"

"Don't remind me." He stopped massaging my head and shuddered.

"I'm not sure why you're upset," Kate said. "I'm the one who fell on top of her dead body."

"Who do you think has to do her hair for the funeral?" He turned away from me and started rubbing Kate's head vigorously.

"You're kidding." I sat up halfway in my chair. Fern pushed me back down with one hand.

"Well, I did the woman's hair for almost ten years. They want to make sure she looks good for the viewing."

I wiped some water out of my eye. "Is this something you normally do?"

"The older my clients get, the more time I spend at the funeral home working on dead heads." Fern wasn't known for sugarcoating his words. "I should open a second salon there."

"Who called you about doing her hair?" Kate asked.

"Her best friend, Beverly. They've both been coming to me for years."

"Really?" I started to sit up again, but Fern had a hand on my head. He pumped some shampoo onto my hair, and I heard him doing the same to Kate.

"They were in the salon just a few days before the wedding. This is the mango and chamomile blend to invigorate the scalp. They wanted me to hide their roots."

"I guess they're not natural blondes?" Kate didn't sound surprised. We had watched the women who came out of Fern's salon get blonder by the year.

"Half the 'natural' blondes in this town are my work. Now I'm putting on a coconut and papaya conditioner."

"You're making me hungry. Annabelle wouldn't let me eat a thing today."

I ignored Kate's whining. "So then Mrs. Pierce and Bev were getting along the last time you saw them together?"

"Of course." Fern rinsed my hair with a burst of freezing cold water. "This will make your hair shine."

"Had either one started acting strange recently?" I tried to dance around my real question.

Fern squeezed my hair and twisted it up into a towel. "Not that I noticed. Why all the questions?"

"For God's sake, Annabelle." Kate sat up, holding her towel around her head. "She's wants to know if Clara knew that her husband and Bev were having an affair."

"Oh, is that what you're asking?" He pushed us up with a finger on our backs and guided us to two plush red stylist chairs. "She knew about the affair for ages. I thought you were hinting at something big."

"You don't call that big?" I stared at Fern as he towel-dried my hair with one hand and Kate's with the other.

"You have to understand these society tramps." Fern held up a long, wet strand of my hair.

I tried not to let my mouth fall open. I had never gotten used to the way Fern referred so casually to his clients.

"I just tell it like it is," Fern smiled at my surprised look. If I called my clients tramps, I'd be fired. Fern managed to insult people with a big smile on his face and get tips for it. "I think we should do soft layers around your face and get rid of this ridiculous blunt cut."

I tried to sound nonchalant. "As long as I can still pull it up."

"What's the point of having a fabulous haircut if you always wear it in the ponytail?" He started cutting. I closed one eye.

Kate swiveled her chair around to face Fern. "I don't get it. Didn't having an affair with Dr. Pierce give Bev the leg up on Clara?"

"So to speak?" Fern elbowed Kate. "That's not the way Clara saw it. See how these layers frame your face, Annabelle? I don't suppose you'll let me do high-lights, too?"

"Don't push it."

"Clara got bored with her husband." Fern measured two sections of hair along my jawbone. "She only married him to get back at her ex, anyway."

"This is getting juicy." Kate rubbed her hands together.

"Dr. Pierce and Dr. Harriman were best friends about seven or eight years ago, girls. Clara found out her husband . . ."

"Dr. Harriman at the time, right?" I asked.

Fern bobbed his head up and down. "He cheated on Clara with one of his nurses. Huge scandal."

"That must have burned her up." I brushed a pile of wet hair clippings off my lap. "Especially since she's so into people's status in society."

"She wanted revenge." Fern ran a hand through my hair and gave an approving nod. He turned to Kate. "What's the best way to get even with a cheating husband? Have an affair with his best friend, Clara thought."

"I hope you didn't give her that advice," I said.

Fern put a hand on his hip. "I would never meddle in someone's personal life. Anyway, that's not the best way to punish a cheating man."

I didn't wait to hear Fern's way. "She did more than have an affair with him, though. She married him."

Fern shrugged. "Clara could overdo it sometimes."

"You don't have to tell us about Mrs. Pierce going overboard." I ran a hand through my hair. I'd have to remember to check the scale later. I'd probably lost at least a pound in hair weight.

"By the time Clara finished getting revenge, she'd married a nice doctor. But that was it." Fern flipped Kate's head forward.

"What do you mean?" I took off my smock and shook the hairs into a gold trash can by my feet.

"Clara loved money, glamour, and power. Her new husband had money, but nothing else that mattered to her. After a while she got bored and just ignored him. I'm going to angle the sides to give you movement, Kate."

"Poor Dr. Pierce." Kate peeked out from under her long bangs. "No wonder he had an affair with Bev."

"Who could blame him?" Fern held a section of Kate's hair up and measured it with a shining, gold comb.

"He certainly had a motive for murder," I said.

"There are two things I know, girls. Hair and men. That man didn't have the guts to kill her."

"What about Bev?" I sat back down in my chair and spun around. "Could she have killed her best friend?"

He brushed the back of Kate's neck with a fluffy brush. "I wouldn't put the murder past her, but why bother? Clara knew about the affair with her husband and didn't care."

"I'm still not quite clear on why she didn't care." Kate examined the back of her hair with the gilded hand mirror Fern handed her.

"Simple. She had her own little fling to distract her."

I nearly fell off my chair. "Someone was willing to

have an affair with that witch?"

"You didn't know?" Fern seemed gleeful. "With the president's top economic advisor."

"Do you mean the one who's on the news a lot?" I could hear my voice begin to shake.

"She's the kind of woman who likes to trade up," Fern nodded, and then pulled out a blow dryer with a long nozzle. "You know the one, right? He's got just enough gray at the temples to look honest. Boyd, I think."

"William Boyd." Kate met my eyes in the mirror. "Oh, we know him all right."

I could feel a knot forming in the pit of my stomach. "We were just hired a few weeks ago to plan his daughter's wedding."

Chapter 14

"So Mrs. Pierce had an affair with a prominent political figure who just happened to hire you. Why didn't you tell me sooner?" Richard had been waiting when Kate dropped me off in front of my building. I'd revealed the latest development in the Pierce soap opera before we even reached the second floor.

"What are you talking about? I just found out about it myself," I insisted.

"Not about the affair." Richard led the way up the narrow staircase. "I mean about being hired by the Boyds. Were you trying to keep it a secret so you could use another caterer?"

"Don't be so paranoid. We were both too caught up with the Pierce wedding to think about anything else. To be honest, I intended to set up a tasting with you as soon as we were through." I stopped at the top of my landing. Nearly a dozen crates and cardboard boxes were stacked around my doorway. A pile of plastic garment bags slid off one of the boxes and onto the floor. "What in the world is going on?"

Richard shifted from one foot to another. "I had the equipment that I took from police storage delivered here. I figured it would be more practical that way."

"Why would it be more practical to keep your cooking equipment here? Why not at your catering kitchen?"

"I don't want anyone to get the wrong idea, since I'm still technically closed and can't use the company kitchens." Richard started pushing one of the boxes forward as I opened the front door.

"When you say that you took the equipment from the police, am I to assume that this is legal?"

"Are you suggesting that I stole my own equipment from the police station?" Richard looked as outraged as he could manage while straining behind the weight of a large brown box. "They gave me everything they no longer needed for the investigation and made me promise not to open my kitchens until the exact cause of death has been determined."

I picked up a milk crate and placed it inside the door. "Why am I getting an uneasy feeling about this?"

"I can't imagine." Richard wouldn't meet my eyes.

"I do have an idea I wanted to run by you, though."

"I knew it." I slid another box inside my apartment with my foot.

"Since I'll be staying here until things are safe again, why not do my catering from your kitchen?" Richard scooped up an armload of plastic garment bags.

"Wait a second." I shook my finger at him. "I thought you weren't allowed to cater."

"They asked me not to open *my* catering kitchens." Richard pushed the last box through the doorway by crouching over and getting a running start of a few feet. He stood up and brushed off his hands. "They didn't say anything about using *your* kitchen."

I closed the door and threw my keys on the nearest end table. "I won't have to worry about being killed. You're going to get me arrested first."

"Arrested for what? Illegal flambé? Possession of an unlicensed spatula?" Richard dismissed my concern with a flick of his wrist. "Don't be silly. There's nothing to worry about."

"What happens when the police return and see your little setup?"

"What reason would the police have to come back here?" Richard pulled out what appeared to be an industrial-strength chrome blender from one of the boxes. He disappeared into the kitchen, and then opened the white, wooden shutters that divided the top half of the two rooms and poked his head out. "This counter would be a perfect breakfast bar if you got rid of all this junk."

"That's where I put my mail. I haven't gone through it in a while." I flopped down onto the chair facing the kitchen. "Reese said he'd return the guest list some-time, so I think you can count on him getting a glimpse of your covert operation."

Richard scooped my piles of junk mail and overdue bills into his arms and vanished behind the counter. "He needs to drop something off, right? We'll make sure he doesn't come in the kitchen. That's simple enough."

"This plan is destined for disaster," I moaned.

"I have only a few small parties, anyway. Nothing we can't handle."

"We?" I gaped at Richard. "I hope you mean you and your invisible friend."

"You're so heartless, Annabelle." Richard's voice cracked. Such a faker.

"I'm already harboring a criminal activity, so don't even dream about getting me charged with aiding and abetting, too."

"They don't send people to jail for cooking, darling." Richard popped his head out of the kitchen. "Do they still wear stripes in prison? I would look atrocious in horizontal stripes."

"I think they wear blue now." I rolled my eyes.

"I look fabulous in blue." Richard sprayed the counter with cleaner and wiped it away with an exaggerated swipe. "Especially if it's a deep, electric blue. Accentuates my eyes."

I stared at the pile of garment bags that Richard had

dropped on the couch. "Let me guess. You even brought uniforms for us to wear."

"That's not a bad idea, but no." Richard stuck his tongue out at me through the space above the counter. "Those are the bridal party tuxedos that you're supposed to return to the shop. I put them in my car the other night and forgot about them until today."

I glanced at my watch. "Well, it's too late to return them now. The place closes at five."

"I would've returned them for you, honey, but I wasn't sure which tuxedo place you used."

I let my hair down. "Don't worry about it."

"Well, knock me over with a feather boa." Richard rushed into the living room and pretended to stagger against the wall. "You finally cut that mop."

"Thanks, I think," I said as Richard recovered from his shock and began examining my hair from all angles. The phone rang while he fluffed the back of my hair with his fingers, and I grabbed it from the coffee table.

"Miss Archer, this is Mike Reese. Detective Reese. We've made a copy of the guest list you loaned me, so I thought I'd return it to you tonight."

"That's fine." I looked at the boxes of contraband taking up most of my living room. "When should I expect you?"

"I'm already in Georgetown, so it shouldn't take me more than five minutes."

"Perfect." I cursed Richard silently. "See you in five minutes."

I clicked off the phone and tossed it behind me on the chair. Richard held a pocket mirror up so I could see the sides of my hair he had teased straight out. I glared at him. "Detective Reese is on his way and if you don't want me to break down and make a full confession, you'd better do something with all this stuff."

Chapter 15

The doorbell rang, and I glanced over my shoulder into the open kitchen where Richard stood amid his neatly arranged supplies. He wore a plaid apron edged in pleats that we'd found wedged in the back of a drawer. "Are we ready?"

"Absolutely." Richard waved a metal spoon at me. The smell of sautéed onions filled the apartment. Richard had found a withered onion sprouting roots in the back of one of my refrigerator drawers and cut it into pieces. Hopefully the detective wouldn't get close enough to notice the lack of any other food. "Just making dinner and minding my own business."

"Good." I paused before opening the door. "Try not to talk too much."

Detective Reese wore a pair of jeans that were broken in. He slipped off a brown leather jacket, and I tried not to notice how great his arms looked in the white T-shirt underneath.

"It sure smells good in here." He walked toward the kitchen. "What are you cooking?"

I opened my mouth, and then went completely blank. Richard and I hadn't planned that far.

"A sweet onion tart with goat cheese." Richard looked up from the stove. My stomach growled. Leave it to Richard to pull something out of the air and make it sound delicious.

"It's an experimental recipe." I didn't want the detective to get any ideas about staying for dinner. "We don't know if it'll be any good."

Reese leaned on the counter separating the living room and the kitchen. "I didn't know that the owners of catering companies actually cooked. I thought you had chefs."

"We have several chefs." Richard puffed out his chest. "But you have to know the basics, in case of an emergency."

"Is making dinner for a friend considered an emergency?"

"This is more of a favor," Richard explained. "An emergency is when your chef calls in sick."

"Or when you aren't allowed to use your staff or your kitchens?" Reese leveled his gaze at Richard.

A flush began to creep up Richard's neck. He punched the fan button on the range. "It's getting hot in here."

"Can I offer you anything to drink?" I stepped between Reese and the kitchen, remembering my empty refrigerator as soon as I'd spoken. Please let him not be thirsty.

"No, thanks." Reese turned from the kitchen, seemingly satisfied that he'd scared Richard enough. He sat on the edge of the couch and pulled the folded guest list from his jacket. "We didn't have any luck finding anyone named Phillips on the master list. Chances are that isn't even important, but we're grasping at straws right now."

"Do you have any suspects?" I sat down across from him and watched as he flipped through the list.

He studied me for a moment. "I shouldn't be discussing this with you."

"I'm only asking because I might be able to give you some information you don't have." I cleared my throat. "About some people who aren't upset that Mrs. Pierce is dead."

"From what we've discovered, that won't narrow down the field much." Reese grinned and dimples appeared in both cheeks.

I tried to stay serious. "I just found out that her husband and her best friend were having an affair, and Mrs. Pierce knew about it."

Reese's eyes widened. "Interesting. Are you sure?"

"I saw it with my own eyes." I blushed, and then shifted my gaze away from him. "You know what I mean."

"I know what you mean." He pulled out a pad of paper and a silver pen. "What's the best friend's name?"

"Bev Tripton. Also write down William Boyd."

Reese tapped his pen on the table. "That name sounds familiar. What's the connection?"

"He's the president's economic advisor, and Mrs. Pierce was having an affair with him."

"I won't even ask how you got this information, Miss Archer. You shouldn't be running around playing detective."

"I have no desire to do your job for you, Detective." I crossed my arms tightly in front of me. "All I care about is clearing Richard's name."

"Him?" Reese lowered his voice to a whisper and jerked a thumb behind us where Richard leaned over the counter trying to listen. "We don't consider him a real suspect."

"Then why the big deal about examining his equipment and testing his food? You know all this bad publicity is ruining his business."

"We're not trying to put anyone out of business, but we are trying to solve a murder."

"So now you're sure Mrs. Pierce was murdered?"

"You don't read the papers, do you?" Reese cocked an eyebrow at me. "The article that ran this morning leaked the fact that an overdose of two different kinds of blood pressure medications killed the victim."

"Two kinds?" I had to start reading the newspaper.

"Mrs. Pierce took one medication for high blood pressure, but we found two drugs in her system. One was her prescription and the other wasn't."

I winced. "I guess it's what you'd call too much of a good thing."

"I guess so." The detective gave me a brief smile. "So now we have to determine how the killer delivered the second medication to her."

"By slipping it in her food or something?"

"That's what we're hoping to find out by testing the leftover hors d'oeuvres and plates for residue of the drug." The detective pocketed his notebook, and clicked the silver pen a few times before standing.

"Couldn't she have accidentally taken the wrong medication?" I followed him to the door. "How can you be sure it's murder?"

"It's unlikely that she would have taken two types of pills within a few hours. We checked her prescription and her pill box. No sign of the second medication."

"Which means that someone else knew what medication she took and mixed the two on purpose."

Reese put a hand on my arm. "I appreciate the names, Miss Archer, but let the police do the investigating."

"I'm not trying to . . ." I started, but the detective cut me off.

"Stick to wedding planning." He grinned and gave my arm a small squeeze. "It's less dangerous." What a condescending jerk!

"That's what you think." I pulled my arm away and swung open the door, making a point not to meet his eyes.

"Thanks again." He gave a wave to Richard, and then stepped into the hallway. He caught the door with one hand as I tried to slam it shut and leaned close to me. "By the way, Annabelle, I like your hair."

Chapter 16

I stood in front of the bathroom mirror after my morning shower and studied my haircut. A bad idea. I could never make my hair look as good as Fern did when he cut it. I always spent one day looking great and three months pulling my hair up so I didn't have to attempt to style it. I blew my hair out and attempted to style the smooth layers. Hadn't the ends turned under yesterday?

"Since when do you use a blow-dryer?" Richard poked his head in the bathroom, rubbed his eyes, and then stepped in to stand behind me. He'd slept in the khaki pants and white T-shirt he had on last night.

"Since I got this high-maintenance haircut." I crimped the ends with my hands. "I'm going to have to quit my job to keep up with it."

"That's the price of beauty, Annabelle." Richard yawned and covered his mouth. "Were you planning on using the kitchen this morning?"

"What do you think?"

"Right. Stupid question." He walked back down the hall.

"What's on the menu for today?" I called out.

Richard had brought in bags of groceries the night before and filled the refrigerator and cabinets. My kitchen must still be in shock.

"Just a couple of drop-off lunches for law firms." His

voice carried down the hall. "Pesto chicken on focaccia, espresso-rubbed steak salad, fruit with a tarragon glaze. That kind of thing."

I abandoned the bathroom—and any hopes of my hair behaving—and joined Richard in the kitchen. I hoisted myself up on the counter next to the sink and let my feet swing from side to side.

"I just cleaned that, honey." Richard motioned to the Formica counter. He opened the refrigerator and started to pull out cellophane bags.

"I guess there's no chance of getting breakfast around here?" I pawed through the bags he put next to me. All produce. Not my idea of comfort food.

"Do I look like I'm running a diner?" He slapped a Styrofoam package of meat in the sink, then thrust a paper bag in my direction. "I had a feeling this would happen, so I stopped in the bakery section last night."

I peeked in the bag and sighed. "Blueberry muffins with a crumb topping. I'm in heaven."

"I hope this means you'll be staying out of my way?"

"You bet." I slid down off the counter. "Kate and I agreed to do a little more snooping around, so as soon as she gets here . . ."

"I forgot." Richard snapped his fingers. "Kate called while you were drying your hair to say that she's going to be late."

"How late?"

"She didn't say. Something about going to visit a former boyfriend who works at the White House and getting more information about Boyd."

"Very late." I took a muffin out of the bag and bit into it, sending bits of sugar onto the floor.

"Weren't you just saying last night how you needed to catch up with client calls and paperwork?" Richard ignored my mumbled complaints about Kate as he pushed me out into the hall. "Now is your chance."

I finished the first muffin before I reached my office. Peering in the bag, I stepped gingerly over the favor boxes on the floor and sat down at my desk. Only two more muffins. I had to make them last. Richard wouldn't be happy if I came back for more food.

I opened my phone log and started dialing clients. Voice mail on the first three calls. I tried to make most of my client calls early in the morning or around lunch time, so I could leave a message and not get stuck in hour-long conversations about bridesmaid shoes. Since it was morning, I hoped everyone had gone for a coffee break.

"One more thing I forgot." Richard reached an arm around the door frame, without showing his face. He dropped a piece of paper with a phone number on my desk. "Mrs. Boyd called while you were doing your hair."

That settled it. I would never blow-dry my hair again as long as I lived.

"Anything else you've forgotten to tell me, Richard?" I raised my voice as he scurried back to the kitchen. "Like all my brides have decided to elope?"

I dialed Mrs. Boyd's phone number and counted the

rings. After the sixth ring an out-of-breath voice answered.

"Mrs. Boyd?" This didn't sound like the perfectly put-together political wife.

"Yes?" she snapped. "Who is this?"

Oh, no. Not another Mrs. Pierce. I didn't remember her being like this when we met.

"Annabelle Archer from Wedding Belles. I'm returning your call."

"Of course, Annabelle." Mrs. Boyd's voice warmed up. "Thank you for returning my call so promptly. It's been a little crazy around here."

"I understand." I hoped she couldn't hear my sigh of relief.

"I called you to talk about selecting a caterer." Mrs. Boyd rustled papers on the other end of the phone. "Now that we've booked the Meridian House for the reception, I hoped we could set up some tastings."

I glanced down at my calendar. "When would be good for you?"

"I know it's short notice, but anytime this week. Next week my husband goes out of town, so if we don't fit it in soon we'll have to wait until the beginning of next month."

"I might be able to get a caterer to do a tasting for you this week. That way we can get the process started."

"Could you?" Mrs. Boyd sounded pleased. "That would be perfect. We want a caterer who does French food well. We want this wedding to have the feel of a garden party in Provence."

"That won't be a problem. There are some fabulous toile linens that would be lovely for cocktails outside."

"As long as they're pink. We want everything to be pink."

I winced. "Everything?"

"Everything," Mrs. Boyd said. "Even the food needs to match."

Great. The wedding would look as though it had been hosed down in Pepto-Bismol. I walked with the cordless phone to the kitchen and waved my arms to get Richard's attention.

"What are you doing tomorrow night?" I mouthed to Richard.

"Nothing," he whispered back. "Why?"

I walked back to my office. "I'm certain that Richard Gerard Catering would be willing to do a tasting in your home tomorrow night."

"He's supposed to be wonderful, isn't he?" Mrs. Boyd said. "Are you sure he'll agree to such a short notice?"

"I'll handle it," I assured her. "I'll have him put together a menu today and fax it over to you."

"Don't forget our color scheme, Miss Archer."

I thought such rigid color schemes had gone the way of color-coordinating the bridesmaids with the punch. I heard Richard coming down the hall as I said good-bye to Mrs. Boyd.

"What are you up to, Annabelle?" He stood outside my office door, hands on his hips.

"Since you're so gung-ho to cater, I figured you wouldn't mind doing a tasting for Mr. and Mrs. Boyd tomorrow night." I spun all the way around in my office chair. "It'll give us the perfect opportunity to see how much Mrs. Boyd knew about her husband's affair, and if Mr. Boyd had anything to do with the murder."

Richard drummed his fingers on his hips. "And how do you expect to get this information out of them? Should I plan on putting truth serum in the food?"

"I guess I'll just see how they react when I casually mention Mrs. Pierce. People usually give themselves away when they're lying."

"I'm going to go to all the hassle of throwing together a last-minute tasting just so you can see if you get a reaction?" As the doorbell rang, Richard turned on his heel and stomped down the hall. "That detective got it right, Annabelle. You should leave the investigating to the police."

I followed him to the living room. "You might get a catering job out of this, too. It's not a total waste."

"Maybe you can talk some sense into her," Richard said to Kate as he let her in. He appraised her acid-green skirt slit up to midthigh. "Maybe not."

"And wait until you hear what I found out about William Boyd." Kate tossed her hot pink plaid purse on the couch.

"Wait until you hear what she's gotten us into." Richard jerked a thumb in my direction.

"You go first, Kate." I perched on the arm of the

116

couch and let Kate stretch out across the rest. That skirt was too tight to sit up in.

Richard went back into the kitchen where we could watch him through the open shutters. "I hope you don't mind if I listen from in here. Not all of us can spend all day playing private eye."

"Somebody is in a lovely mood." Kate kicked off her heels.

"Ignore him," I said. "Tell us what you found out."

"So I went to the White House to visit Jack, that guy I used to date last year. Do you remember me talking about him?"

"The one who laughed like a girl?"

"No." Kate propped her head up against a cushion. "The one who had a shoe fetish."

"I think so." I needed a chart to keep them all straight.

"Anyway, I paid Jack a visit this morning. We had a great time catching up and swapping work stories. We even set a date for dinner tonight."

"Please tell me this is going somewhere," Richard said, his voice muffled behind a cabinet door.

"It just so happens that his office is only a few doors down from Boyd's and he filled me in on some pretty interesting fireworks that went on last week."

"Mrs. Pierce?" I leaned forward.

"You got it." Kate swung her legs off the couch and inched herself into an upright position. "Jack didn't hear anything specific, but he said Clara did plenty of yelling when she visited Boyd."

"I wonder what they were fighting about." I stood up and paced the room.

"The rumor around the office is that she must have threatened to tell his wife about their affair. What else could it be?"

"That would do it." Richard heaved a chef's knife up and it landed on the cutting board with a thud.

"No one heard exactly what they fought about, but everyone heard what Boyd said after Clara left." Kate stood up and walked behind the couch to lean over the counter into the kitchen.

I couldn't believe she would tease us like this. "Well, what did he say?"

"Jack said that Boyd fumed all day and stalked around the halls saying that Clara wouldn't get away with it, and that he would shut her up once and for all."

"Anything else?" Richard eyed Kate.

"Just that he would kill that meddling bitch." Kate grinned. "That's all."

"Bingo," I said. "I think we've found our murderer."

"Just because he threatened to kill her?" Richard gave a little snort. "If I remember correctly, darlings, you both made similar threats."

"We weren't serious." I walked to the counter and grabbed a strawberry when Richard turned away. "But if Clara had been about to ruin our lives by exposing a secret, maybe we would have been."

"She ruined my life for a while," Kate said under her breath.

"People make idle threats, then get over it all the

time." Richard returned to the big, glass bowl of fruit salad and pursed his lips. He glared at me. I stopped chewing and tried to swallow the berry whole. How could he miss a single strawberry?

"Water under the ridge," Kate said.

"Bridge," Richard and I said simultaneously.

"Most likely a lover's spat." Richard moved the salad bowl to the other side of the kitchen. "They probably forgot about it long before the murder."

I wiped my mouth on my sleeve and ignored Richard's disapproving glare. "When was the fight?"

"That's just the thing. They wouldn't have had time to forget about it," Kate said. "It happened the day before the wedding."

I whooped. "See, I told you the tasting would be a good idea."

"What tasting?" Kate asked.

"The one I arranged for Richard to do at the Boyds' house tomorrow night. It'll be the perfect opportunity to sniff out more clues."

"This is getting much too Nancy Drew for my taste," Richard griped.

"They won't know we're there to find information. Mr. Boyd could never expect us to know that he threatened Mrs. Pierce's life the day before she was killed. I don't think even the police know that." I winked at Kate. "What were the chances of you dating someone who overheard all this?"

"With Kate, I'd say the odds weren't bad." Richard blew Kate a kiss.

"Ha, ha." Kate turned her back to Richard and flounced back to the couch. "I wouldn't mind getting to snoop around inside their house. It looks amazing from the outside. Not that I'm thrilled about the idea of hanging around a murderer. If Boyd did do it."

"I'd be willing to bet that he had something to do with her death." I tapped a finger on my chin. "And tomorrow night will be the perfect opportunity to find out."

Richard glanced up from slicing pieces of focaccia and rolled his eyes. "What could possibly go wrong with this plan?"

Chapter 17

"Everything that could possibly go wrong today already has." Richard polished a sterling silver knife with the dishtowel tucked into the waistband of his pants, then placed it on the Boyds' long, mahogany dining table. Everything about the room, from the floors to the walls to the claw-foot table, was dark wood.

"That's good." I set an oversized pink-rimmed base plate in front of each of the tall chairs. "If nothing else can go wrong, then dinner will be perfect."

"First, I couldn't get the grade of filet I wanted. I had to settle for choice." Richard set a ruler on the table to see if the silverware was even on both sides of the plate. "Then Party Settings delivered the wrong dessert plates. Wait until you see them. They look like hospital china, which means I'm going to have to paint the plate with raspberry coulis to cover it up. And, of course, I couldn't find the wine that matched the pink peppercorn sauce anywhere in the city."

"Remember that this tasting is just so they can sample your food. This isn't the final menu for the wedding." I patted his arm. "I think you've done an amazing job considering the short notice I gave you."

"I'm almost positive that this is the least amount of time I've ever had to pull together a formal dinner," Richard snipped. "No other caterer would dare to try."

"You get full marks for bravery." I set a white plate with a scrolling pattern on top of the charger. Classic and formal, yet not boring. Richard considered matching people's personality and tableware an art form.

"I'm not the brave one. You're trying to catch a murderer. Where do you think he is, anyway?"

We hadn't seen anyone since Mrs. Boyd let us inside two hours earlier. I glanced at the grandfather clock in the corner. Half an hour left before we were scheduled to start the tasting.

Kate wedged an ivory taper into the crystal candelabra in the middle of the table. "Didn't you hear Mrs. Boyd say he had a doctor's appointment right before this?"

"I bet we have time to snoop around a little before he gets here," I whispered.

"Snoop around?" Kate almost dropped her handful

of candles. "That's not part of the plan."

"Mr. Boyd's office is right across the foyer and the door is partly open." I tugged at Kate's arm. "If we're going to do this, let's do it right."

"You're nuts." She pulled away from me. "What if he comes home early and we get caught?"

"Doctor appointments always run late, so there's no way that Boyd will get here on time," I assured her.

"What if Mrs. Boyd comes back downstairs?"

"That's why Richard's going to stand guard for us." I looked tentatively at Richard.

"Leave me out of this." Richard started out of the dining room, and I ran to catch him. "If you think I'm going to be around when you two get hauled off to jail, you're out of your mind. I'll tell you where I'll be. Crawling out the kitchen window."

"Please, Richard. Kate and I will only poke our heads in for a second."

Richard allowed himself to be prodded across the foyer.

"After two minutes, you're on your own," he huffed.

"Stand out here and if you hear anyone coming, give us a signal." I pushed the door to Mr. Boyd's study open the rest of the way.

"Would a flare suffice or were you thinking more along the lines of exotic bird calls?"

I gave Richard my most saccharine smile. "A tap on the door will do nicely."

We stepped into the office, and I could make out the shape of a desk in the corner. I heard Kate sliding her feet across the floor, probably so she wouldn't trip, and I did the same. We reached the desk and Kate turned on a lamp sitting on the edge. I snapped it off.

"What are you doing?" I blinked hard, temporarily blinded by the light. So much for my eyes having adjusted to the darkness.

"How are we going to find anything if we don't have light?"

"Let's try this." I felt my way over to the window and found the plastic bar that adjusted the blinds. I twisted it, and stripes of soft moonlight fell onto the desk.

"Not bad." Kate bent over the desk and picked up a book. "His calendar."

I took it out of her hands. "I wonder why he doesn't have it on him."

"Maybe he keeps one for here and one for the office. Flip to the week before the wedding."

"What's taking so long, girls? Hurry it up."

I cursed Richard under my breath for making me jump. "Two more minutes."

"I'll give you one, and then I'm out of here," he hissed back.

Great. No pressure. I flipped back a page in Boyd's calendar and ran my finger down the record of meetings.

"This guy visits the doctor a lot. He had an appointment last week, too."

"Is Clara's name in there anywhere? Or the initials CP?"

"Not that I can find." I scanned the pages quickly.

"Feel around. Is there anything else on the desk?"

"Ugh. I think he emptied his pockets on here. Stick of gum, a few pennies, receipt, ball of lint."

"Where's the receipt from?"

Kate uncrumpled it. "From a pharmacy. For a prescription."

"I wonder what he takes. Does it have a date?" Kate unfolded it. "The tenth."

"The day of the wedding. Are you thinking what I'm thinking?"

"That I can't believe this guy picks up his own prescriptions?"

"Good point." I tried not to sound too surprised as I took the receipt from Kate. "But he would pick it up himself if he didn't want anyone to know about it. Mrs. Pierce died from mixing two blood-pressure medicines, right? What if the prescription Boyd had filled the day of the wedding was for one of them and he somehow used it to kill her?"

A sharp rap on the door made my stomach drop.

"That's Richard's signal." Kate clutched my arm. "We've got to get out of here."

Chapter 18

A high-pitched, warbling whistle followed Richard's loud tap on the door.

"Is that supposed to be a bird call?" I stuffed the drugstore receipt into my shirt pocket.

"Who knows?" Kate whispered. "I'm not waiting around to see if he sends up a flare."

I held out my arm to stop Kate from barreling through the door when I heard Richard's voice, much shriller than usual.

"This is the most breathtaking parquet floor I've ever seen, Mrs. Boyd."

I held my breath. They sounded as if they were right outside the door.

"Why, thank you, Mr. Gerard."

"Call me Richard. Everyone does."

Footsteps indicated they were heading away from the office door.

"If you have a minute, Mrs. Boyd, I'd love to show you the china we chose for this evening. I think of it as Martha Stewart meets Louis the Fourteenth."

I cracked the door. "Okay, Kate. It's all clear. Richard has Mrs. Boyd in the dining room with her back to us."

"Where are we supposed to have been?"

"There's a powder room under the staircase. We could be coming out of there."

"Both of us?" Kate asked. "Together?"

"Better she thinks we're weird than she finds us snooping around her husband's office."

"If you say so."

We tiptoed past the dining room, and then made a big production of shutting the door to the bathroom and walking loudly down the hall.

"There you are." Mrs. Boyd turned as Kate and I entered. A petite woman with dark hair cut in a thick page boy, Helen Boyd had a tight smile that seemed to blink on and off again like Christmas tree lights.

"Did we miss anything while we were washing up for dinner?" I asked.

Richard gave me a fake smile. "All we've done so far is review the menu."

"I hope you found the bathroom without any problem, Miss Archer."

I waved her concern away with one hand. "No problem at all. I love the way you've decorated it."

She raised an eyebrow. "Really? Most women don't like the fly-fishing motif."

Fly-fishing? I should have checked out the bathroom before opening my big mouth.

"Annabelle isn't most women." Kate patted me on the back. "She adores fly-fishing."

"Do you, now?" Mrs. Boyd studied me carefully. "Then you and my husband will have lots to talk about. It's his passion."

"You know I'm more of a beginner, Kate." If looks could kill, I'd have been in the market for a new assistant.

"He'll be thrilled that someone speaks his lingo. Heaven knows I don't share my husband's fondness for the outdoors." She bestowed a series of her blinking smiles on us.

Richard looked at his watch. "Are we expecting Mr. Boyd soon?"

"Yes, but why don't we get started without him?" Mrs. Boyd lowered herself into the chair that

Richard slid out for her.

"Excuse us for one moment." Richard let me and Kate walk past him into the kitchen. "We'll be back with the first course."

Kate waited until Richard closed the door before collapsing in a fit of giggles. "Good luck chatting with Mr. Boyd about fly-fishing."

"Who decorates their bathroom with a fly-fishing motif?" I leaned over and let my head fall on the wooden kitchen island, glowering at Kate from my inverted position. "You're pure evil squeezed into a Lilly Pulitzer dress."

Richard waved his hands like a bird about to take flight. "Fight it out later, girls. You haven't told me if you found anything in the office yet."

"We found something all right. Show him the receipt, Annie." Kate only used my nickname when trying to get on my good side.

I produced the slightly crumpled yellow copy for Richard to inspect.

Richard took it from me. "He fills his own prescriptions?"

"That's what I said." Kate wore a look of vindication as she opened the lid of the stainless-steel stock pot simmering on the stove.

"Am I the only person paying attention here?" I snapped my fingers. "He fills the prescription, then attends the wedding. Mrs. Pierce dies of an overdose of blood-pressure medication. Hardly a coincidence."

"The sneaky and suspicious side of your character is

really coming out, Annabelle." Richard pushed Kate out of the way, and stirred the contents of the pot. "I like it."

"I've got to agree with Annabelle, it's all too convenient," Kate said. "If Clara planned on exposing their affair to his wife, causing her to leave him, and possibly ruining his political career, I'll bet he'd do anything to stop her."

I nodded. "If they'd been seeing each other, he'd know that she took blood-pressure medicine. It wouldn't take a genius to figure out that giving her a big dose of blood-pressure medicine on top of her own medication would kill her."

Kate rubbed her hands together. "We know he had plenty of motive. He had opportunity, too, because we saw him at the wedding. I'll bet he pulled her aside to apologize for the fight, and then managed to slip her the poison."

"Now we have evidence." I took the receipt and tucked it in the zippered compartment of my purse. One piece of paper I didn't want to lose.

Richard lifted a wooden spoon from the pot and took a taste from it. "We can prove that he got a prescription filled, but we can't be sure that it was the same medication they found in Clara's system."

"I just have a feeling, Richard. The case is coming together."

Kate rocked on the balls of her feet. "Just to play devil's adjective, how did he get a doctor to prescribe it to him?"

"It's devil's advocate." Richard pointed the spoon at Kate.

"What if he takes blood-pressure medicine himself?" I said. "It wouldn't be unusual among political types."

"We can find out if he has high blood pressure." Richard lifted the pot off the stove and set it in the sink.

"Let me guess, Kate and I will sneak up to his bathroom and go through his cabinets?"

"I thought of simply asking his wife. Unless you two didn't get your fill of spying?"

"How are we supposed to work that into casual conversation?" I put my hands on my hips. "Please pass the pepper and the blood-pressure pills, if you have any."

"You'll figure something out, Annabelle." Richard ladled a spoonful of pale pink soup into a shallow bowl and passed it to me.

Kate took two bowls and put her back against the door. "If not, you always have fly-fishing to fall back onto." She backed out of the kitchen, smirking.

I followed and set a soup bowl in front of Mrs. Boyd, then sat down across from Kate. "Since your daughter's wedding will be next summer, Richard chose an apple chestnut soup to start the meal." Inspiration struck me. "We can lower the amount of salt in case either you or your husband have any health concerns. Like high blood pressure?"

"We both have mild hypertension, but nothing to be concerned about for the wedding."

Jackpot.

"Do you take medication?" I asked.

"Yes, why?" Mrs. Boyd eyed the soup and didn't make a move toward her spoon.

Kate gave a forced laugh. "Don't let Annabelle worry you. She likes to get a full family profile when we start the planning process. Allergies, likes, dislikes, medications."

"Am I too late? Did you start without me?" Mr. Boyd came through the front door, dropping his square brief-case in the foyer and continuing into the dining room. Kate sent her soup spoon clattering onto the table.

"Not yet." Mrs. Boyd turned her cheek when her husband bent down to kiss her.

I'd remembered Mr. Boyd as being taller and more handsome when we'd had our first meeting. I could see why women would be attracted, though. Chocolate brown hair with a distinguished amount of gray. Blue eyes that any woman would die for. Discovering that he'd killed my former client in cold blood lowered his overall sex appeal, though.

"We were just about to taste the soup." I pushed my chair back and almost flipped it over. "Let me get you some."

Richard had a filled soup bowl in his hand when I stepped into the kitchen. "Was that Mr. Boyd I heard?"

I nodded. "He's our guy. Mrs. Boyd told us he takes medication for blood pressure. He's the killer." My heart pounded. I needed some blood-pressure medicine myself.

"Okay, Annabelle. Calm down. Maybe we should call the police and let them take over from here."

"Not until after the tasting," I insisted. "Maybe he'll let something slip and incriminate himself even more."

"Fine. But if anything happens, remember that I'm right in here with 911 predialed on my cell phone and my finger on the send button."

Not exactly how I pictured the cavalry arriving, but I could live with it.

I nudged the door open with my toes, and carried the bowl with both hands. I lowered it in front of Mr. Boyd and noticed he'd drained his water glass. "Apple chestnut soup served warm with a dash of crème fraîche."

"Helen cooks like this all the time." He winked up at me. "Right, honey?"

"I would if you were ever home."

"I guess I've held back my wife's cooking ability all these years by working late." Mr. Boyd laughed and took a spoonful of soup.

Mrs. Boyd stared into her soup, stirring it in circles.

"This is one of Richard Gerard's signature warm weather dishes." I felt the need to fill the silence. "It's just crisp enough to be refreshing, but substantial enough for a formal dinner."

Mrs. Boyd didn't stop stirring and didn't look up.

"Could I get a little more water?" Mr. Boyd strained to swallow. I hoped the soup wasn't too thick.

I reached for the silver water pitcher on the side-board behind me, and Mr. Boyd held out his crystal goblet for me to fill. Mrs. Boyd's eyes flashed as she watched her husband gulp down the entire glass and resume eating his soup.

"We can also serve it in a demitasse cup if you'd prefer to have six or seven smaller courses," Kate offered. I mouthed a quick thanks for the save, and forgave her for the whole fly-fishing incident.

"That's a thought, Helen." Mr. Boyd put his spoon down, leaving a small pool of pink in the bottom of his bowl. He cleared his throat. "Like the tasting menu we tried at Citronelle."

Mrs. Boyd's voice became a hiss. "I've never been to Citronelle."

Mr. Boyd stood up halfway, knocking his chair to the ground. His hands gripped the table on either side of him, and I saw red blotches creeping up his neck. It looked as if he would explode. Kate's mouth dropped open, and I made a slight motion with my head that we should leave.

As I tried to slide out of my chair without being noticed, Mr. Boyd gasped for breath, his mouth opening and closing like a fish. His arms began to shake, and then he collapsed on the table, his face completely in his soup bowl.

Mrs. Boyd let out a piercing scream and Richard burst through the door, cell phone in hand.

We all stared at Mr. Boyd, purple faced with pink drops of liquid in his hair.

"It's the soup!" Mrs. Boyd turned on Richard, waving her finger viciously. "You've killed him! You've poisoned my husband."

To his credit, Richard didn't faint.

Chapter 19

"Well, we can cross Mr. Boyd off our suspect list." I sat next to Kate and Richard at the end of the Boyds' living room sofa, staring at the intricate pattern of the Persian carpet covering the floor. We were waiting for Detective Reese to return and finish questioning us. He'd been called away to talk with Mrs. Boyd before her Valium kicked in.

Richard sat with his head in his hands. "I still don't understand how this happened. At least at the wedding there were lots of people who could have murdered Mrs. Pierce."

"I know." Kate rubbed her temples. "Tonight, we were the only ones in the house, aside from Mrs. Boyd."

I crossed my legs and jiggled my foot in circles. "Mrs. Boyd is the obvious suspect, considering how irritated she seemed to be at her husband, but did you see how shocked she looked when he fell over?"

"You can't fake hysterics like that." Kate pulled her dress down an inch.

"He could have had a heart attack or something." Richard sounded hopeful.

"With all these cops crawling around taking pictures and questioning us?" I shook my head. "Unlikely."

The door across from us opened, and Detective Reese strode across the room. In a dark gray blazer over black pants and a tightly knotted striped tie, he looked far more official than he had the other night when he stopped by my apartment. And far more severe.

"Let me see if I understand this correctly. All three of you thought it would be a good idea to set up this dinner and use it as some sort of trap?"

Richard barely met the detective's eyes. "I wouldn't say trap, exactly."

"What word would you use, Mr. Gerard?" Reese paced in front of us. I had to uncross my legs so he wouldn't hit my foot. "Enlighten me."

I cleared my throat. "We wanted to see how Mr. Boyd would react if we brought up Mrs. Pierce and the murder. Casually."

Reese glanced at the notes he'd made earlier. "You thought he might be the killer because of a fight he and Mrs. Pierce had the day before the wedding, right?"

I could hear sarcasm dripping from his voice. Okay, it didn't sound like such a great reason when presented like that.

"We believe she threatened to tell his wife about the affair," Kate said in a tiny voice.

"That's the only evidence you had?"

We all nodded. We'd told the police what Kate learned from her White House source, but we'd omitted the evening's illegal search-and-seizure operation in Mr. Boyd's office. Our fabulous clue that sealed the case against Boyd seemed useless now. No need to tell the police since we'd dropped Boyd off our suspect list for good.

Reese closed his eyes and rubbed them with one hand. "Each time I turn around, Miss Archer, I find you in some sort of trouble with one or both of your side-kicks."

Richard twitched at the word "sidekick." I elbowed him. "I'm sorry, Detective. I'm not trying to get in these situations. Honestly."

"I asked you to leave the detective work to me. Now I'm ordering you. Stop running around trying to solve this thing on your own."

"Okay." I stared at my lap. I felt awful. We'd only made things worse.

"I hope you realize this is dangerous stuff you've gotten yourself into." Reese touched a hand to my shoulder. "I don't want to see you get hurt."

My face flushed, and I didn't lift my head to look at him.

He pulled his hand back. "I don't want to see any of you get hurt."

I didn't raise my eyes until I heard Reese pull the door shut behind him.

Richard stood up. "I don't know about you, Kate, but I'm a little upset that our safety came as an after-thought."

"You're reading too much into things, as usual." I shook my head.

"Can we get an expert opinion on that, Kate?"

"Definitely interested," Kate confirmed. "Although I

don't know why, considering the way she treats him."

"What do you mean?" I went to check that the door had closed all the way.

"You don't give him any encouragement at all. How is he supposed to know that you like him?"

"I don't like him." I tried not to raise my voice. I didn't want Reese to overhear.

"Sure you don't, Annie." Richard came over and put an arm around me. "You always blush when you speak to a man."

"Why not tease him a little?" Kate walked across the room twisting her hips like Marilyn Monroe. "Like I do."

"I don't think tease is an accurate description for what you do," Richard muttered.

Kate stuck her tongue out at him. "Then it'll work perfectly for Annabelle."

"I'm not going to tease the poor guy, so you two can forget about it."

"Fine, have it your way." Kate walked back to us minus the twist. "People will start talking about the wedding planner who can't find a husband for herself."

"I'm not searching for a husband." My face got warm again. "I don't want to settle for someone just for the sake of getting married."

"I didn't say you had to settle," Kate said. "But you know what they say, a bird in the hand is worth two bushes."

I opened my mouth to correct her, then stopped.

"Why would Annie need to get married when she has

us?" Richard winked at me. If he meant this to be comforting, it didn't work. I thought about what Kate had said and wondered if I should stop focusing on work. Everyone else in the world was getting married. At least it seemed that way to me. My phone began singing and I pulled it out of my purse, glancing at the number on the caller ID. Kimberly Kinkaid. I hoped she wasn't calling about pinning flower petals to the grass again.

"Hi, Kimberly. What can I do for you?"

"What do I do with my purse during the reception?"

I could feel my eye begin to twitch. "What do you mean?"

"Should I put it on the table or under my chair?" Hysteria began to creep into her voice. "What is proper wedding etiquette?"

I was sure Emily Post didn't have a section in her book on purse placement. I tried not to sound irritated. "It's fine to put it next to your chair."

I could hear her let out a deep breath on the other end of the phone. "Okay. I can check that off my list now."

Detective Reese stuck his head back in the door. "Mr. Gerard, I just remembered something."

"I've got to run, Kimberly," I whispered into the phone, then dropped it back in my purse.

Richard raised a hand to his mock turtleneck. "Yes, Detective?"

"I left a message on your voice mail, but I'll go ahead and save you the trouble. We finished analyzing all your equipment and testing the food from the wedding. It's clear that the poison came from a source unrelated to your food, so we gave the go ahead for you to reopen your business."

"Thank you, Detec . . ."

"In light of Mr. Boyd's murder, though, you can disregard that message."

My mouth fell open. "You're sure he was murdered?"

"We're sure. We'll focus our investigation on the obvious . . . the soup."

"Mr. Boyd was poisoned, too?" Kate gulped.

Reese closed the door without another word. So much for our inside source. Richard turned slowly to face me.

"This is all your fault." He jabbed a finger at my nose. "I'm not listening to any more of your brilliant ideas."

"Calm down, Richard."

"I will not calm down. I'm going to end up in San Quentin. I'll spend the rest of my days cooking in the prison cafeteria for people called Tommy One Thumb and Sammy the Weasel."

"You're not going to be arrested." I dodged his finger, which came closer and closer to my face. "Your soup had nothing to do with Mr. Boyd's murder. If he was poisoned, it must have happened before he arrived home. Maybe someone slipped something into his drink at work."

"Stop trying to figure it out." The vein on the side of Richard's head pulsed. "That's how we got into this mess in the first place."

"If I recall correctly, you were just as into solving Mrs. Pierce's murder as I was."

Kate tried to get between us. "She's right, Richard. We both made the decision to try to find Clara's killer."

Richard marched to the door. "If I hear one more word about anyone trying to solve anything, there will be more than two bodies for the police to worry about."

He slammed the door behind him, and Kate turned to me. "He really got his toes out of joint, didn't he?"

Chapter 20

"So, did the same person kill Mrs. Pierce and Mr. Boyd?" Kate slowed as we reached the front of my building and looked over her shoulder. The small market across the street had closed, and the streets were dark and quiet.

"It seems too coincidental for both of them to die within days of each other." I found my keys and opened the heavy front door. The tiny foyer held a silver grid of mailboxes and the staircase. No room in Georgetown for a fancy lobby. I checked my mailbox quickly, and then put a finger to my lips. "Don't make any noise. I saw the lights on in Leatrice's apartment."

We started tiptoeing up the stairs, and Leatrice appeared in the hall.

"Don't worry about disturbing me, Annabelle." Leatrice wore a brightly colored peasant dress and what appeared to be a red tissue paper flower in her hair. "Just watching an old episode of *Murder, She Wrote*."

"Sorry to be in such a hurry." I didn't stop climbing. "We've had a long night. We're too tired and hungry to stop."

"Not a problem, dear. I'll tell you what. I'll order us a pizza, and you can tell me all about your night." Before I could protest, she'd run back in her apartment, and I could hear her on the phone.

"This is the perfect end to an already horrible night." I bent forward and dangled my arms over the railing.

"If she's buying, I can put up with a little chatter for a while." Kate shrugged. "It'll be like being on a bad date."

I managed a smile. "You always know how to put a positive spin on things. At least we won't have to worry about her trying for a goodnight kiss."

"I'm not so sure. She seems to like you an awful lot, Annabelle."

Leatrice bounced out of her apartment and pulled the door shut. "The pizza will be here in twenty minutes." She held up a kitchen timer. "If they're late, it's free."

I led the way upstairs with Kate behind me, and with Leatrice and her ticking timer bringing up the rear. If only I could tag Leatrice with one of these, I thought, then I'd always hear her coming.

I pushed open the door to my apartment and let Kate and Leatrice walk in first.

"Good heavens!" Leatrice dropped her timer and the

buzzer went off prematurely. Richard stood in the middle of the living room in a pair of purple silk draw-string pajama bottoms and nothing else. He had a trim waist any woman would covet, and I couldn't help wondering if he waxed his chest or if his skin was really that smooth.

Richard flung his arms over his bare torso. "It's considered polite to knock before barging into a room."

"It's my living room," I protested. "I wasn't aware I had to knock."

Richard picked his pale green angora blanket off the floor and wrapped it around his chest. "I thought it would be easier to stay here tonight and move my things in the morning."

"You don't have to leave." I tried not to sound exasperated.

Richard pulled the blanket up to his neck. "When I'm around you, bad things happen to me."

"I'm sorry I got you in trouble, Richard. But listen, Kate and I have figured out how someone could've murdered Mr. Boyd before he came home."

"Murder?" Leatrice sounded excited.

"I can't believe what I'm hearing." Richard let the blanket slide back down to his waist. "Let me guess. You've concocted a brilliant plan to catch the real killer by throwing a brunch that, of course, I'll cater. We'll assemble all the suspects and then they'll all start dropping dead. Poisoned, naturally."

I rolled my eyes. "I see that you're still upset."

"Why would I be upset?" Richard shrieked. "I'm

only under suspicion for murder for the second time in one week. Both your clients, I might add."

"Things seem bad now, but you'll be cleared in this death just like you were for the last one."

"Not another word!" Richard pursed his lips and held his palm up to me. He turned to Kate and Leatrice and gave a dignified bow. As dignified as you could be with an angora throw wrapped around you. "If you'll excuse me, ladies. I'm going to bed."

"Come on, Richard. We've ordered a pizza." Kate picked up Leatrice's timer and handed it to her. Leatrice just stared at Richard with her mouth agape.

"No, thank you. I'll be on the bedroom floor trying to get some sleep before the police come and drag me away." Richard flounced off down the hall.

Leatrice took my hand and squeezed it. "I don't think things are going to work out with this one, dear."

"He'll get over it." Kate dropped onto the couch. "You know what they say . . ."

"Don't, Kate. I can't handle anything else being murdered tonight, even words."

"What kind of fight did you have?" Leatrice asked.

"Not a fight, exactly." I sat down next to Kate. "He blames me for getting him in trouble with the police."

"The police? Did you see that cute detective again?" Leatrice seemed torn between her love of mysteries and her need to find me a husband.

"Yes, Detective Reese happened to be at the scene of the crime." Did everybody I know have a one-track mind?

"The scene of the murder, you mean?" Leatrice's whole face lit up, then she squeezed my hand. "That detective is just the type of man you need, Annabelle."

"You're not the only one who thinks so," Kate said to Leatrice. The doorbell came to my rescue.

Leatrice frowned at her broken timer. "I think they took more than twenty minutes, but I can't prove it."

I got the idea Leatrice ate a lot of free pizza.

"I'll get drinks for all of us." I walked to the kitchen while Leatrice paid.

"Don't bother." Kate took a six-pack of Coke from the delivery man.

"I ordered drinks, too," Leatrice said. "I've seen the inside of your refrigerator, remember?"

Kate cleared a space on the coffee table for the pizza and drink cans while I brought a stack of LIZ AND JAMES cocktail napkins from the kitchen and passed them around. Leatrice handed me a steaming slice of pizza, its trails of cheese hanging underneath like loose string. I thought back to the last pizza I'd tasted at a client's wedding. Thin, the size of a silver dollar, topped with goat cheese and frisée. I took a bite of the gooey sausage-and-green-pepper pie and sighed. Now, that was more like it.

"You were telling me about your run-in with the police," Leatrice reminded me, dabbing at her mouth with a napkin.

"One of our clients died tonight at a tasting Richard did for us." I tried to talk through a mouthful of cheese.

"Another client?"

"You make it sound like they've been dropping left and right."

"Well, they have been," Leatrice said a little too cheerily. "How did this one die?"

"It appears to be poison, again." I popped open a can of Coke and took a sip. "Unfortunately, that means that they're looking at Richard's soup as the cause of death."

"He blames Annabelle because she came up with the idea to do the tasting in the first place." Kate picked at a blob of cheese stuck on the inside of the pizza box. "That's why he's madder than a wet pen."

Leatrice nodded at Kate with a puzzled expression on her face.

I barreled on. "I don't think the death had anything to do with our tasting. I think we were just in the wrong place at the wrong time."

"It doesn't look too good to be involved in back-to-back murders." Leatrice pressed her eyebrows together. "That's an awfully big coincidence."

"We're aware of that, Leatrice," I said.

Kate turned to me. "I think you're right, though. Mr. Boyd had such a violent reaction to the poison it must have been something strong. Something that toxic would have smelled so bad he wouldn't have eaten it."

Leatrice's face lit up. "If he was poisoned sometime before the tasting, it could have happened to take effect after he ate the soup. Do you know where he was before he came home?"

"When we looked in his day planner, I didn't look at

144

today's schedule." Kate shook her head. "I focused on what he did the week of the wedding."

Leatrice dabbed at her mouth with a napkin. "Were you girls snooping around?"

"Just a bit," Kate admitted. "We thought this guy who died might have been the person who killed our first client, so we were looking for clues."

"Don't you remember, Kate?" I snapped my fingers. "Mr. Boyd had a doctor's appointment right before he came home. My money says he reacted to something he was given then."

Kate threw her pizza crust back in the box. "Why would his doctor poison him, though?"

Leatrice picked up Kate's crust. "Is he with an HMO?" Kate and I both gave Leatrice a look.

She shrugged. "Well, that would explain it, dears."

"Maybe his doctor didn't poison him," Kate said. "Lots of people have reactions to medicines."

I dropped my half-eaten slice onto the table. "What if the doctor thought that Mrs. Pierce told Boyd something she shouldn't have? There are two doctors I can think of who might have benefited from Mrs. Pierce's death."

"What are the chances that Boyd goes to one of them?" Kate leaned back on the couch.

Leatrice didn't blink. "Who?"

"It's worth checking out," Kate said as if she'd read my mind.

"Dr. Pierce and Dr. Harriman." I tossed my balled-up cocktail napkin in the pizza box. "The husbands."

Chapter 21

"I'm leaving you, Annabelle." Richard stood in the doorway of my bedroom. "I've packed up my things in the kitchen, so your apartment is back to normal."

I sat up in bed, rubbing my eyes. "You're not still mad about last night?" Everything that happened at the Boyd's house rushed back to me. If only it had been a bad dream.

"About the murder you managed to make me the chief suspect for?"

I managed a weak laugh. "I'm sure Reese wasn't serious about that."

"Right, Annabelle. Policemen always joke around at crime scenes. It's part of their charm." Richard turned on his heel and stomped down the hall. I jumped out of bed to follow him.

"Come on, Richard," I begged. "Don't leave like this."

"You're clearly insane if you think I'm going to stick around and get sucked into another harebrained idea that might get me killed or worse . . . sent to prison."

"How could I predict that Boyd would drop dead? This isn't my fault."

Richard flung open the door. "Your idea to do the tasting. Your fault."

"Not my idea to serve soup," I said under my breath.

"I heard that, Annabelle." Richard rolled up the

sleeves of his yellow linen shirt in precise folds. "The soup tasted divine. I sampled it myself."

"See? The soup couldn't have been poisoned." I hid behind the door in my tattered red flannel pajamas. Not something I wanted anyone to see.

"Try telling it to the police. On second thought, don't tell anything to the police."

"Maybe I could convince them that you had nothing to do with Mr. Boyd's death if we proved that he'd already been poisoned when he ate the . . ."

"Stop right there." Richard put his arms out like someone bracing for impact. "Don't talk to the police. As a matter of fact, don't talk to anyone. Especially me. Don't call me. Don't write me."

I sighed. "Richard, you're being ridiculous."

He bent to pick up a box. "If it's ridiculous to want to go one day without being accused of murder, then I'm guilty as charged. You're a trouble magnet. Stay away from me." Richard marched to the top of the stairs and tossed his head back. "Good-bye forever, Annabelle."

I felt as if I were stuck in a gothic novel.

"Come on." I ran after him as he disappeared down the stairs. "Don't go away mad."

Richard sniffed. "I'm going to go where no one can hurt me anymore."

"And where would that be?"

"The Red Door Salon. The one at Fairfax Station next to the Louis Vuitton store." He choked back a sob. "But don't even think of following me."

Oh, for crying out loud. Most of my break-ups with boyfriends hadn't been this dramatic. Halfway down the stairs I remembered the torn seat of my pajama pants and ran back up to my apartment. I listened to Richard's footsteps getting farther away. Fine, if that's the way he wanted it. I started to slam the door when I saw Leatrice's head popping up behind the railing of the staircase.

"I couldn't help overhearing." She walked up to my landing, breathing heavily. For an old lady, she had incredible hearing.

"Come on in, Leatrice." She would, anyway. I slammed the door shut and hoped Richard could hear.

"Don't be upset, dearie. To tell the truth, I've seen this coming for a while."

So much for Leatrice's keen perception. "Richard and I just work together. No romance between us, I promise."

"I thought he'd been staying over." Leatrice moved the plastic tuxedo bags to sit on the couch. I'd forgotten to return them for the fourth day in a row. I hated paying late fees.

"Just as a friend. So I wouldn't be afraid to stay here after the break-in."

"He brought so many things with him, I thought maybe he'd moved in with you."

Who needed a neighborhood watch group when you had Leatrice keeping tabs on you?

I kept my hand over the rip in my pajama bottoms and walked sideways to the kitchen. "Do you want coffee?"

148

"Not if it's that instant kind," Leatrice grimaced. "I came up to see if you and Kate are planning to question the two doctors today."

"We're going to do a little investigative work at Dr. Harriman's office, but other than that we're keeping a low profile. We don't want people knowing we're still snooping around." I poured the contents of a Nescafe single into a mug. "If Detective Reese questions me one more time, I think he might put me in protective custody."

Leatrice beamed at me. "Protective custody with the detective. That doesn't sound so bad."

I moaned and turned on the electric kettle. That morning I needed coffee to deal with Leatrice.

The phone in my office rang and I looked at the kitchen clock. Ten o'clock. Damn. I'd bet the messages were piling up. If I didn't return their calls right away, my clients would send out a search party. The kind with torches and pitchforks. I skidded down the hall in my socks and grabbed the phone on the third ring, managing a breathless hello.

"Did you get the fax of the cake sketches?"

"Hi, Alexandra." I flipped through the pile of faxes that sat in the machine. "I'm glad you're not a crazed bride."

Alexandra laughed. "I sent them to you and the Murphys yesterday. I wanted to know if you'd heard from Mrs. Murphy yet."

I found the cake sketches and sat down at my desk. "I haven't checked my messages this morning. Yesterday turned out to be a bit hectic."

"Another deadly client?"

I winced. "You could say that. Okay, I'm looking at the cake designs."

"Do you think I made the bow cake too hideous?"

I studied the drawing of a tall, tiered cake with what appeared to be giant tongues rolling down from the top. "I think it's safe to say she won't choose it."

"Mission accomplished." Alexandra sounded pleased with herself.

"There's my Call Waiting. I'll let you know what Mrs. Murphy says about the cake."

I clicked over to the other line, half expecting an irate Mrs. Murphy to be screaming about bows.

"What a sexy voice, Annabelle."

Who was this? A pervert who knew my name? I cleared my throat. "Can I help you?"

"It's Maxwell Gray."

The photographer from the Pierce wedding. Famous for photographing society brides and hitting on anything in a skirt. Except his brides. Bad for business, he said.

"Right. How have you been?"

"Swamped with nothing but calls from people wanting to hear about the Pierce murder. I haven't gotten any work done. What have you been up to?"

Setting traps for suspects, sneaking around people's houses for clues, witnessing a client's death. "The usual."

"I wanted to tell you that I rushed the proofs from the

wedding. I thought the bride would like to have the portraits of her mother as soon as possible. If you want to look at them before the bride and groom pick them up later this afternoon, stop by the studio."

Most photographers sent me sample pictures for my portfolio, but I didn't always get a chance to see the photos before the client. I hoped Maxwell didn't have any ulterior motives. "Thanks. I'd love to see how the museum photographed. Kate and I have an appointment first, but how about I swing by in a couple of hours?"

"I'll be waiting."

Technically snooping around Dr. Harriman's office with Kate couldn't be considered an appointment, but I shrugged off my little white lie. Seeing the wedding pictures would be just the thing to take my mind off the murder case for a while. And Richard claimed I couldn't stay out of trouble. What did he know?

Chapter 22

Kate swung into a parking space in front of the Chevy Chase Cardiology Center, missing the car next to her by mere inches. "So what's the plan again?"

I flipped my phone shut, feeling less guilty about doing more investigating. I'd spent the entire drive to Dr. Harriman's office on my cell phone with brides and felt completely caught up. I knew that feeling would last five minutes at the most.

"Simple," I explained. "We go into the office and you make a scene to distract the receptionist while I sneak into the records room and see if Dr. Boyd is a patient."

"What kind of scene?"

I slipped on a pair of sunglasses. "Anything you want, as long as it's dramatic."

Kate sighed. "We need Richard for something like this. He's the best at faking illness."

"Well, he's not talking to me at the moment, so we'll just have to manage without him." I opened the car door and tried to wedge myself out in the tiny sliver of space Kate had given me.

She stood waiting for me behind the car when I'd finally managed to squeeze out. "Maybe I should go in ahead of you so I can have time to create the distraction, and you can slip by me."

"Sure." I nodded and brushed the dust off my pants. It looked as if I'd polished the entire side of the car with my legs. "The next time I'm going to be the wheelman."

We walked to the front of the steel office building, and I watched Kate go through the revolving glass doors. I looked at my watch and cursed in my head. We should have synchronized. For all I knew, Kate could have run into a cute security guard and not even have been past the front lobby by then.

I watched another couple of minutes tick by and decided to go inside. I found Dr. Harriman's name on the directory in the lobby and got on the elevator to go to the fifth floor. As soon as I stepped off the elevator, I heard Kate's raised voice. Good old Kate. Her distraction sounded very distracting. I felt bad for ever doubting her.

I opened the door to Harriman's offices and met with a verbal outburst so loud I almost ran back out. Kate stood at the receptionist's desk punctuating each sentence with a string of curses.

"Ma'am, we're a cardiology practice." The receptionist looked as if her patience was wearing thin. "We can't help you with your Tourette's syndrome."

My mouth almost fell open. Perhaps I should have been more specific about the type of distraction. At least all eyes were on Kate.

I slipped through the waiting room and into the back offices as Kate yelled something about spanking. I would have to give the girl a raise.

I walked down the hall passing three examination rooms and a men's bathroom. Where did they keep their files? I rounded a corner and froze. Dr. Donovan stood at the end of the hall, but he appeared to be studying a patient's chart and didn't see me. I took a few steps backward and ducked into the men's bathroom I'd just passed.

I didn't want to try to explain what I was doing creeping around his offices without an appointment. Not to mention why my assistant had a sudden onset of acute Tourette's syndrome in his waiting room. I groaned to myself thinking of Kate creatively swearing up a storm. I had to get us out of here.

My cell phone began ringing, and I dove into my purse for it. I flipped it open and held my breath. I didn't hear anyone in the hall, but I could hear Richard nearly shrieking on the other end of the phone.

"I'm a little busy right now, Richard," I whispered, cupping my hand over my mouth to muffle the sound.

"That's what I hear," he snapped.

"What are you talking about?" I couldn't believe I was arguing with Richard over the phone while hiding in a men's bathroom.

"I went back to your place to make amends and apologize for being a bit sensitive this morning . . ."

"You're forgiven, Richard." I cut him off. "Now can I call you back later?"

"But Leatrice said that you and Kate took off out of here like a shot talking about finding evidence." Richard's voice went up a few octaves. "I know you're not out there getting into more trouble after all that's happened."

I heard voices in the hallway getting closer, and I stepped into one of the stalls and pulled the door closed behind me. "Of course not, Richard."

"Please tell me you have more sense than to get yourself in even deeper trouble than you have already, Annabelle."

I stepped onto the toilet seat and crouched down so my head didn't poke above the stall. My slingbacks would be a dead giveaway if anyone walked in and saw my feet under the door. "Give me a little credit."

"Then why are you whispering?"

I gulped and thought for a second. "Kate and I are at a museum. You know I can't talk normally when I'm in a museum."

"Why are you in a museum?" Richard sounded skeptical. "Which one?"

"The National Museum of Women in the Arts. We're doing a walk-through with a bride."

Richard was silent for a few seconds. "Does she have a caterer?"

I grinned. Always the businessman. "Not yet, but I promise you can do a proposal."

"This doesn't mean I'm not still angry with you," Richard said with a huff. "But send me the information and I'll work on something for your bride."

He hung up, and I let out a deep breath. I had to get out of there before I got arrested and Kate got dragged off to the mental ward.

As I stepped down off the seat with one foot, the strap of my other slingback slipped off my heel and the entire shoe dropped into the toilet. Damn. Damn. Damn. I fished my shoe out with one finger and dropped it on the floor, then opened the door to the stall and looked around the bathroom. Two gleaming metal hand dryers were mounted on the walls with not a paper towel in sight. Why was I not surprised?

I slid my foot into the dripping shoe and leaned against the door, listening for voices. Nothing. I poked my head out of the bathroom. The coast was clear. I squished down the hall and dashed through the waiting room, where a group of irritated nurses surrounded

Kate. I caught her eye as I slipped out the door and motioned for her to follow me.

I held the elevator until Kate got inside, the two of us breathing as though we'd run a race. We didn't speak until we were out of the building and in the car.

Kate put the key in the ignition and turned to me. "Well, did you find anything?"

"No," I shook my head. "I ran into the groom before I could find the files."

"What was he doing here?" Kate stared at my feet. "And why is your shoe leaking?"

"You don't want to know." I gave a shudder. "Donovan shares a practice with his father-in-law, remember?"

"I'd totally forgotten." Kate slumped over the wheel. "So all of that was for nothing?"

"Well, it wasn't a total waste." I took a deep breath. "I learned a few new colorful words."

Kate gave me a sideways glance. "Now what?"

"Well, you still have your meeting with Jack from the White House, right?"

Kate perked up. "You're right. Maybe he'll be able to tell me something good."

"You're going to be subtle, right?" I put on my seat belt as Kate flung the car in reverse. "We don't want word getting around that we're trying to solve this case."

Kate winked at me. "I'm always subtle."

I swallowed hard. "Just drop me back at the office so I don't have to watch."

"What are you going to do while I'm pumping Jack for information?"

"I got a call from Maxwell Gray this morning. The pictures from the Pierce wedding are in, so I'm going to look at them before the bride and groom pick them up."

"You're going to see pictures of Clara right before she died? How creepy."

"I didn't think of it that way. I figured we spent enough time planning the wedding. We might as well get some shots of the decor for our Web site."

"Just be careful you don't get more than you bargained for," Kate warned. "You know photographers in this city."

"Not as well as you do, I'm afraid."

There were few straight men in our business and they all seemed to be photographers. Kate had dated enough of them to have learned to keep her distance. She arched an eyebrow. "Take my word for it, then."

"Don't worry, Kate. Everything will be fine."

"Why does that sound familiar?"

Chapter 23

My cell phone rang, and I hunted for it on the passenger-side floor as I merged from M Street onto the Key Bridge. By the time Kate had dropped me off at my car in Georgetown, I was already running late to meet Maxwell. I'd thrown my purse in the front seat and half the contents of my bag had spilled out.

I had one hand on the wheel and one groping among the loose papers on the floor where I'd last spied my phone. I heard the rings slide under the passenger seat and into the back. Reaching behind me, I scooped up the phone, keeping one hand on the wheel. A car honked as I veered into its lane for a moment. Almost as bad as Kate's driving.

"Wedding Belles. This is Annabelle." Office calls were being forwarded to my cell phone, so I wouldn't get too far behind with work.

"Are you at Maxwell's?" Kate asked. I heard car horns around her, and knew she must be in traffic, too.

"Not yet." I took a right off of Key Bridge onto the GW Parkway. The thick green trees created a lush corridor for me to drive through. The perfect day for a convertible. Not that I didn't love my old Volvo, but I dreamed of being less practical. "How's your meeting with Jack?"

"I'm running a little late. I'm not sure how much more he can tell me about Boyd, though. Unless the man ran up and down the halls announcing the name of his doctor, this might be pointless."

"See what you can find out. I'm just curious."

"Don't tell Richard. He'll have a fit."

"This isn't the same thing as snooping. You're just chatting with an old friend." I accelerated on the gentle curves of the road, and then looked out my passenger-side window. A crew team practiced in the Potomac River, their boat cutting the smooth water.

"I don't think Richard would see it that way. Had he calmed down this morning?"

"Not exactly." I shifted the phone to my other ear. "He told me never to contact him again."

"Don't worry, Annabelle. He'll cool down in a day or two, and life will be back to normal."

"You're probably right." I didn't tell her that I'd dialed his number twice, before remembering the Annabelle embargo, and hanging up.

"Call me when you're done at Maxwell's studio. And be careful, Annie."

"I doubt the murderer is after me, Kate."

"I'm talking about Maxwell."

I laughed, turned off the phone, and tossed it on the seat next to me. Maxwell Gray proclaimed himself the ladies' man of the wedding industry. Not that he had a lot of competition. He looked like a cover model for a romance novel, only older and much more weathered. I didn't consider his silk-shirt-and-gold-medallion-brand of sexiness much of a turn-on, although I'd heard I was in a minority among my colleagues. I cringed at the thought.

I almost missed the exit for the Chain Bridge and had to brake hard not to fly off the sharp curve of the ramp. Too busy thinking about Maxwell and his conquests. I glanced at the directions in my lap to make sure I hadn't passed his studio. I drove by the entrance to the CIA and continued through the primarily suburban area until I came to a cluster of office buildings. I turned into the parking lot and found a space in front of Maxwell Gray Photography.

His studio had large front windows filled with portraits of brides in various dramatic settings. How had he convinced a bride in her wedding gown to lie down in the middle of a wheat field? Most of my brides were afraid a ride in a limousine would wrinkle their dresses. Forget rolling around in a field.

I walked into the studio. A chime signaled my arrival. Maxwell came around a corner and advanced on me, taking my hand and pressing it to his lips. He wore his ash blond hair long and brushed off his face, the back perfectly smooth. He did a better job with a blow-dryer than I did. He had an unnaturally thin nose, and teeth so perfect they had to have been capped. He ran his tongue across his top lip as he released my hand. The Pierce photos had better be nothing short of amazing, I thought to myself.

"Annabelle, you're as lovely as ever." He gave me a sticky smile and waved me into the appointment room where he met with all his clients. A low glass table held all his sample albums. Two red velvet chairs flanked a royal blue velvet couch. Fringed lamps, perched on a pair of glass end tables, and palm trees filled the corners of the room. I couldn't shake the feeling of visiting a harem.

Maxwell pulled a bottle of champagne out of a standing metal bucket. "Can I offer you a glass?"

"I'm really here to see the pictures. I'm not much of a drinker. Not at eleven in the morning, anyway."

"I thought we might get to know each other a little better."

Perfect. Just when I thought the week couldn't get any worse, the slimiest photographer in Washington starts hitting on me.

I motioned to the ornately framed wall portraits around the room. "Beautiful work, Mr. Gray."

"Call me Maxwell." He poured himself a glass of champagne. Obviously he didn't have a problem drinking before noon. "All the other wedding planners do."

I'll bet they do. I forced myself to smile. "It was nice to finally work with you, Maxwell." And to finally have a client with the budget to afford a society wedding photographer.

"I photographed Clara's family for years. Long before she became a Pierce."

Maybe this visit wouldn't be a total waste, after all. It shouldn't be too hard, I thought, to finesse some information about Mrs. Pierce from him. I wished I'd paid more attention to Kate's flirting instruction.

"I changed my mind about the champagne." I tried to bat my eyelashes, hoping that Kate would be proud. "I'd love a glass."

Maxwell filled a crystal flute with champagne and passed it to me. He raised his glass in a toast. "To possibilities."

The possibility that I won't sue you for sexual harassment. I smiled, and took a tiny sip. Maxwell drained his glass.

"So how long did you know Mrs. Pierce?" I sat down on one of the chairs. He chose the couch and reclined

161

on it so that his black silk shirt fell open to one side, exposing the top part of his chest. I'd never seen such impeccably coiffed chest hair. He must have used mousse.

"I started photographing her family for Elizabeth's sweet sixteen party, so it's been about ten years." Maxwell refilled his glass. "Back when she was Clara Harriman."

"I noticed how well you dealt with her." I pretended to take a drink. "Especially when she got upset at you for taking a shot of her bad side."

"I can be honest with you, right, Annabelle?" He didn't wait for my answer. "That woman made my life a living hell every time I worked with her. If she didn't have so much money and so many rich friends with marriageable daughters, I'd have told her to find another photographer."

"But you never seemed upset."

"I work hard to look so calm . . ." Maxwell chugged his second glass. He noticed my nearly full glass and motioned for me to drink.

When he turned to retrieve the champagne bottle, I dumped the contents of my glass in the base of the nearest palm tree. "So I guess you saw a lot of interaction between Mrs. Pierce and her family."

"If you mean did they all hate her, too, the answer is yes."

I leaned close. "Not her daughter, though?"

"No, not Elizabeth." He spilled a little champagne as he reached over to fill my flute. "And not Elizabeth's fiancé, either. Clara adored him, and who wouldn't like someone who adores you?"

"But everyone else hated her?"

"With good reason." Maxwell turned the empty bottle upside down in the wine bucket. "She ignored her own husband and had made her ex-husband's life miserable when she divorced him. Harriman and his new wife were blacklisted from any important social function for years."

"Which husband do you think had the better motive to kill her?"

He leaned over and put a hand on my knee, giving me what could only be called a leer. "Are we playing detective?"

I slid my knee away from his grip. "No, but I thought that if anyone would be clever enough to figure out who killed Mrs. Pierce, it would be you."

He puffed his chest out, making his abundance of chest hair seem even more prominent. "You're quite perceptive, Annabelle. I do have a theory."

"About which of her husbands killed her?"

"I'd pick Dr. Harriman. Clara enjoyed making him suffer during their divorce. She especially loved spreading rumors about the new wife. I heard the new Mrs. H had to go on antidepressants after hearing that half the town believed she had a love child with a tel-evangelist."

Nothing Mrs. Pierce did shocked me anymore. "I can see how the Harrimans might hold a grudge, but I thought the divorce happened five years ago."

"Clara never stopped spreading rumors to get them ostracized from Washington society. She even refused to invite the new wife to the wedding." Maxwell eyed his empty glass, and his mouth curled into a pout.

"I do remember Dr. Harriman's name being on the invitation alone, but I didn't think anything of it," I said more to myself than to Maxwell.

"No one wanted to cross Clara." He leaned over so far he slid off the edge of the couch and caught himself with one hand. "You should've heard her talking the day she came in to review the group photos she wanted for the wedding."

"About her ex-husband?"

"No, even better." Maxwell licked his lips. "She told me about an affair she'd been having with a political big-wig."

I tried to act surprised. "An affair?"

"The last in a long string." Maxwell got to his feet, swaying as though he stood on the deck of a ship. "Why don't I get us another bottle of champagne? I always keep several chilling in the refrigerator."

I'll bet you do. I waited until he left the room, and then twisted around to empty my champagne into the palm tree for the second time. Poor thing would probably die from alcohol poisoning.

"She bragged about the affair, then?" I raised my voice so he could hear me in the next room.

"She always bragged about the men she fooled around with." His voice sounded muffled and far away. Did he have his head in the refrigerator? "This particular one may have been her best work ever."

"What do you mean?"

"Clara relished having power over people and making them squirm. Some people knit for a hobby, Clara did this." Maxwell's voice sounded strained, as though he were wrestling with the champagne cork. "When I saw her, she told me how upset this guy had gotten when she threatened to go public with the affair."

"So she planned to tell his wife?"

"No, his wife already knew." The champagne cork gave a loud pop from the other room. "Clara wanted to leak it to the media and ruin his political career. Apparently he had aspirations of running for office."

I paused with my upside-down champagne glass over the tree. "Wait a second. His wife already knew?"

"That's what Clara seemed most happy about." Maxwell's words slurred together. "The wife confronted her and made all kinds of threats. Clara laughed about it. Said that dried-up prude didn't scare her."

I dropped my glass and it landed with a thud in the potting soil. Mrs. Boyd knew. This changed everything.

Chapter 24

I hurried to pick the champagne flute out of the dirt and set it on the table. I brushed away a clump of soil before Maxwell returned to the room holding out a new bottle of champagne like a proud father.

"I've been saving this particular bottle for a special occasion." He sat down on the couch and leaned toward me. "I think today qualifies."

Unbelievable. This guy thought he was getting somewhere with me.

"Tell me about the fight that Mrs. Pierce had with Mrs. Boyd." I held out my glass and tried not to look repulsed. "When did it happen?"

"Did I mention the other woman's name?"

Damn! Hopefully Maxwell would think he'd let it slip instead of me. "You weren't supposed to tell me?"

Maxwell ran a hand over his slicked-back hair. "Not that Clara cared, but I've always prided myself on being discreet."

Right. He might as well have put out a newsletter.

I put a finger to my lips. "This will just be between you and me, Maxwell. Our little secret."

His face flushed, possibly from the champagne. "It happened the day before her daughter's wedding. Mrs. Boyd came to Clara's house in the afternoon and made a huge spectacle of herself."

This sounded nothing like the tight-lipped Helen Boyd I'd met. "Why? What did she do?"

"It started out calmly with Mrs. Boyd asking Clara to leave her husband alone."

"Which Mrs. Pierce refused to do?" I prodded.

"Of course." Maxwell adjusted himself on the couch, stretching from end to end. "Mrs. Boyd got angry and called her all sorts of names. Not that any of them were new to Clara."

I smiled, vicariously enjoying the thought of Mrs. Boyd using every name in the book. "How did Mrs. Pierce react?"

"She laughed at the woman. When Mrs. Boyd threatened to tell Mr. Pierce, Clara told her she didn't care. Said she wanted Mrs. Boyd's husband, not her own."

"Ouch. Poor Mrs. Boyd." I picked up my glass of champagne and noticed clumps of dirt floating on the top.

"That's when things got ugly. Mrs. Boyd started screaming that if Clara tried to ruin things she'd kill her."

"Mrs. Boyd threatened her life?"

"Clara didn't take it too seriously, though." Maxwell tipped his glass back to let the last few drops roll into his mouth. "Called her a noisy little mouse and laughed about the whole thing."

I'll bet she's not laughing now.

"Mrs. Pierce told you all of this?" I covered the top of my crystal flute with my hand so he wouldn't notice the dirt.

He nodded, his eyes drooping. "Here we've spent the whole time gossiping about Mrs. Pierce when you came to see my photography."

I'd forgotten about the pictures. I looked at my watch. "I've got a few minutes to spare."

Maxwell pulled a small, square box from under the coffee table with one arm. He barely shifted from his position on the sofa as he handed it to me, then closed his eyes. If I'd finished a bottle and a half of champagne, I'd have felt like taking a nap, too.

"So these are all the proofs?" I took the lid off the box and flipped through the enormous stack of snapshot-size prints. There must have been several hundred photos. No way I could go through them all at once. Maxwell didn't answer me, and I glanced up.

His head lolled to the side and his mouth hung open. Passed out. I put my finger under his nose and let out a sigh of relief when I felt his breathing. I couldn't bear another dead body.

"I've got to be running, Maxwell," I whispered so he wouldn't wake up. "I'm going to take the proofs with me and bring them back later, okay?"

No response. At least I asked. I operated on the philosophy that it's better to ask for forgiveness than permission, anyway.

I walked out on my toes, carrying the box of photos in front of me. When I got in my car, I picked up my phone, pressing the speed dial number for Kate's cell.

"Hi, Annabelle." Caller ID. "Did you escape in one piece?"

"He passed out before he could make his move." I heard the sound of clattering silverware. "Where are you?"

"Hold on a second. Let me go outside." The background noise disappeared. "Jack wanted to take me to lunch, and he's been so helpful I couldn't turn him down."

I tucked the photo box into my oversized nylon purse then backed out of the parking lot and pulled into traffic. "You're a true martyr. Where did he take you?"

"The Palm."

One of the places in D.C. to see and be seen. Kate would fit in beautifully.

"Tough life. Be sure to have the crabmeat cocktail."

"Okay, okay. Don't you want to hear what I found out?"

In my excitement over the Clara Pierce and Helen Boyd fight, I'd forgotten about suspecting one of Clara's husbands of poisoning Mr. Boyd. "Of course."

"Jack didn't know anything about Boyd's doctor, but he said that Mr. Boyd seemed fine when he left work."

"Which gives more strength to our theory that Boyd wasn't poisoned until later." I switched the phone to my other ear. "But I'm not convinced that his doctor killed him anymore."

"I'm not done," Kate said. "Since Jack wasn't any help, I called both doctors' offices. I pretended to be Boyd's scheduler and tried to set up an appointment. Dr. Pierce's office had no record of Boyd, but Dr. Harriman's office did. I made an appointment for Boyd for two weeks from today."

"You're kidding." I merged onto the GW Parkway and got in the fast lane. I couldn't believe it had been that simple to find out.

"Hold on. It gets even better. The police were thinking along the same lines we were."

"What do you mean?"

"They arrested Dr. Harriman an hour ago."

"I don't believe it." I swerved out of my lane for a second, and then grabbed the wheel tightly. "Now I'm really confused."

"What do you mean? It makes perfect sense. He had motive and opportunity for both murders, even if he is handsome."

"I guess you're right. But after visiting Maxwell, I'm not convinced that Harriman is the only one with motive and opportunity." I moved into the right lane to let an SUV pass.

"Spit it out, Annabelle."

"According to Maxwell, Mrs. Pierce told him that she and Mrs. Boyd had a huge fight the day before the wedding."

"About what? I didn't think Mrs. Boyd knew about the affair."

"She knew, all right." The dark SUV stayed right behind me with its lights on. I sped up. What kind of jerk puts high beams on in the daytime?

"That explains why she acted so cold to her husband at the tasting. I wonder if he knew about the fight."

"It happened on the same day that Mrs. Pierce fought with Mr. Boyd. I wonder which came first. Mrs. Boyd's fight might have been the reason that Mrs. Pierce went to see Mr. Boyd. Or maybe, Mrs. Boyd found out about the fight with her husband and went over to have it out."

"It's kind of like the chicken or the leg," Kate said. I rolled my eyes and glanced in my rearview mirror. The

SUV had matched my speed and driven so close to me I could see the driver hunched behind the sun visor. I couldn't make out the face. Too much glare.

I changed lanes. Maybe if I could speed up enough I'd lose this maniac. "Mrs. Boyd threatened to kill her when Mrs. Pierce said she'd expose her husband."

"It sounds like Mrs. Boyd got more upset about her husband's political career being ruined than she did over the affair."

The SUV dropped back and merged into my lane.

"I didn't think of it that way. I guess you're right, Kate. She said something about Mrs. Pierce ruining things. Probably not talking about her marriage."

"I'll bet she's one of these political wives who's put as much into her husband's career as he has. There's no way she'd let another woman take that away from her."

"So much for my bright idea of Mrs. Boyd being the killer. She might have killed Mrs. Pierce, but she wouldn't have killed her husband." I stepped on the gas to try to pull away from the SUV. I passed the rectangular brown sign that informed me the Key Bridge exit was a mile and a half away. Not much farther.

"Who's to say there aren't two murderers on the loose?"

"That makes me feel a lot better. Thanks, Kate." I swerved into the right lane as I drove across a short bridge. I jerked forward as something hit my car from behind. The SUV. "That idiot just hit me."

"What? Are you okay?"

I stayed in my lane as a few cars entered the highway

from the right. "Yeah. I'm going to pull over at the exit for Key Bridge. I don't know what this creep's problem is."

I lurched forward again, this time much harder, and my head hit the steering wheel. The cell phone fell onto my lap, and I tried to pick it up again while the SUV pulled alongside me. I saw the sign for the Key Bridge ahead and sped up. If I could just make it to the exit. I accelerated, driving under a wide concrete bridge, but the SUV swerved into my lane, knocking me off the road. I barely missed going into the concrete bridge, and my car sped toward a patch of tall grass. I screamed, lifted my hands in front of my face, and slammed straight into the Key Bridge sign.

Chapter 25

"I flattened it." I sat up; one hand on my forehead where a throbbing bump had developed. "The sign for Key Bridge is gone."

"Lie back down. The doctor doesn't want you moving, in case you have a concussion." Kate stood next to my bed in the emergency room of Georgetown Hospital. The white curtain had been drawn around us halfway, but we could watch doctors and nurses rush by. Kate looked frazzled. I hated to think how fast she'd driven to get here before my ambulance arrived.

"Thanks for calling 911," I said. "How did you know where I crashed, though?"

"You told me where you were exiting, and then I heard screaming and scraping metal." Kate shuddered. "I put two and two together."

"Is it my head injuries, or did you say that right?"

"You must be delirious." Kate smiled and handed me a paper cup of water.

I leaned back on the thin pillows. "Maybe this is what heaven is like. No mangled expressions."

"Then you must be dying."

A strangled cry came from behind the curtain, and Richard rushed to the bed. He threw himself across my lap. "If you die, I'll never forgive myself."

"Richard, I'm okay. I'm not dying."

Richard lifted his head from the sheet. "You're not? But I heard Kate say you were."

"We were joking around." Kate patted his back. "She's fine, aside from some scrapes and bruises."

"I don't think it's funny to joke about dying." Richard pulled himself up to his full height, and I noticed that his eyes were rimmed in red. He dabbed at his nose.

"We're sorry," I said. "We didn't know you were there. How did you hear about me?"

"Kate called me on her way here. Hysterical. I drove as fast as I could, but obviously not as fast as some people." He elbowed Kate.

"You two didn't have to make all this fuss. I'm fine."

Richard threw up his arms. "Will you stop being so damn independent for two seconds and admit that you need us?"

"Sorry." I reached for his hand. "Thanks for coming. Especially after everything I've done."

Richard's eyes watered. "It's not your fault, Annie. Kate's right. You didn't force me into anything. To be honest, I enjoyed trying to solve the case."

"You did?" Kate raised an eyebrow.

"Not the part where the police put me on the suspect list, but the rest of it was a bit of an adventure."

"I don't mind adventure." I propped myself up on my elbows. "I do mind being run off the road and almost killed."

Richard's jaw dropped. "Run off the road?"

"Not an accident?" Kate's voice sounded unsteady.

"That SUV wanted me dead. The driver didn't just bump my car; he rammed it from the back and the side."

"Who would want to do that to you?" Richard held his fingertips over his mouth.

"Someone who thinks I'm getting too close to finding out who killed Mrs. Pierce and Mr. Boyd."

"But, Annabelle," Richard glanced at Kate. "They already caught the killer."

"Maybe, maybe not," I said.

Kate pulled the curtains the rest of the way around my bed. "You think the murderer is still on the loose and is trying to kill you, too?"

I raised an eyebrow. "Don't you think it's a little coincidental that my apartment gets broken into and I get nearly killed all in the span of a few days?"

"But the police arrested our number-one suspect,"

Kate insisted, perching on the edge of the bed.

"Maybe we were wrong." I looked from Kate to Richard. "Maybe the police are wrong."

Richard patted my hand. "Maybe we should leave well enough alone."

"With someone still out there trying to kill me?"

"Why would the murderer want to kill you?" Kate shook her head. "We've just been playing a guessing game. It's not like you have any hard evidence."

"We might know more than we think. The murderer must be aware that we've been hunting around for clues. Maybe he's scared we'll find something or maybe we already have."

"Annabelle, you could be right." Richard poured himself a glass of water from the plastic pitcher. "We weren't scared when someone broke into your apartment because we thought they were after something."

"Exactly, Richard," I said. "If he didn't find what he wanted, he must assume I still have it."

Kate gave me a weak grin. "Instead of trying to get it back again, he's just trying to get rid of you."

"I must have something that the killer considers a threat. But what?"

Richard tapped his fingers on the metal bar of the hospital bed. "Heaven knows what could be in that mess in your apartment."

"So much for the outpouring of sympathy." I frowned at him.

Richard crumpled up his paper cup. "I think we have two options. We can either take these attempts on

Annabelle seriously and forget about the murders, or we can put all our information together and find out why the killer considers us a threat."

"Everything has happened to Annabelle. Maybe the killer doesn't consider us a threat." Kate pointed to herself and Richard.

"That's fine with me." Richard let one side of his mouth curl up in a smirk.

"Hey," I cried. "What happened to my loyal side-kicks?"

"I think you should make the decision, Annabelle," Richard said. "After all, you're the one who seems to be in the most danger."

I touched the knot on my head and thought about Mrs. Pierce's twisted body and Mr. Boyd's purple face lying in a bowl of soup. "I don't want to let anyone get away with murder."

"Especially when they're killing off our business." Kate winked at me.

"Then we're back on the trail?" Richard went pale behind his smile.

"To be totally honest," Kate admitted. "Annabelle and I were never off it."

"Really?" Richard's smile faltered. "You've been poking around today even after what happened last night?"

"Wait until you hear what Kate and I found out, though."

Richard wagged a finger at me. "You're lucky I'm too happy that you're alive to be mad."

"We've got lots to do." Kate threw back the curtain. "Let's get you out of here."

Chapter 26

Leatrice stood underneath a huge bouquet of helium balloons in my living room. The balloons all read GET WELL SOON in various color combinations and bounced around the ceiling, their ribbons hanging down around Leatrice's face. She wore a necklace made entirely of the little metal bells, and she jingled as she ran to greet me.

"Kate called me and told me about your car accident. I've been worried sick."

I pried her from around my waist. "I'm fine, Leatrice. No major damage."

"The doctor did say you need to rest." Kate led me to the couch. "Your concussion means no running around."

"He said mild concussion."

"A concussion? Oh, dear." Leatrice wrung her hands. "Don't worry. I can stay with you as long as you need me."

I felt a miraculous recovery coming on. "Thanks, but Kate's going to spend the night to make sure I don't slip into a coma or something."

"Well, I'd be more than happy to keep you girls company," Leatrice chirped. "We could stay up all night and watch videotapes of my favorite episodes of *Matlock*."

The coma didn't sound so bad. "How did you get in my apartment, Leatrice?"

"You gave me a spare key ages ago in case you ever got locked out, remember?"

I must have had temporary insanity. "Not really, but it's probably the concussion."

"I wanted to surprise you when you came home from the hospital. Do you like the balloons?"

"They're great." I smiled at Leatrice. "It's not like I stayed in the hospital more than a few hours, though."

"I'm glad they didn't keep you overnight." Leatrice sat on the arm of the couch. "The food at the Georgetown Hospital isn't so good. Now Suburban Hospital has decent food, but I hear the service is terribly slow."

No doubt in the Zagat guide under hospital cafeterias.

"We're not in luck here, either," Kate said from the kitchen. "Looks like a couple of leftover slices of pizza and a few cans of Coke. Is this lettuce?"

Richard walked in the front door that still stood ajar, plastic grocery bags hanging off his hands. "Don't worry. I thought things in your kitchen might be desperate since I cleared out, so I stopped at the store."

He went into the kitchen and began unpacking the bags with Kate. I reached for a cushion, and Leatrice leapt up to put it behind my back. An ideal setup, if my head didn't hurt so much and Leatrice didn't jingle each time she moved.

"Kate mentioned that the car accident may not have been an accident at all," Leatrice said.

"You and Kate had a nice, long chat, didn't you?" I raised my voice to be sure Kate could hear me. She pretended to be busy with the groceries.

"After our pizza party last night, I gave her my phone number. In case she ever needed anything. Good thing I did, too."

"Yeah, good thing." I tried to catch Kate's eye to give her a dirty look.

"So the other car ran you off the road? Were they trying to get rid of you?"

"I don't think you should get caught up in this mess any more than you already are, Leatrice. See where trying to solve these murders got me?"

Her face fell.

"Oh, come on, Annabelle." Kate came from the kitchen and sat on the chair. "Tell her our theories."

"I can help you figure it, too," Leatrice insisted. "I always solve the crime before Jessica Fletcher does."

"See? It can't hurt to run our ideas by someone else." Kate kicked off her heels. "Two heads are better than a nun, anyway."

"Young people today have such colorful expressions." Leatrice giggled and patted Kate on the arm. "I'll have to remember that one."

The thought of Leatrice running around using Kate's garbled sayings made me grin and rub my aching head simultaneously.

Leatrice took a seat beside me. "Do you think the person behind the two murders is the same person who tried to kill you?"

"I'm not sure if the murderer was trying to kill me or just scare me off the trail." I reached for the bowl of personalized candy hearts and popped one in my mouth. My version of comfort food.

"Regardless, your car crash must mean we're getting close," Kate said.

"Who are your suspects?" Leatrice found a pen and legal pad in the piles of papers on the floor next to her feet.

"We keep coming back to Mrs. Pierce's two husbands," I said. "Her ex-husband, Dr. Harriman, who hated her for making his life miserable during their divorce, and her current husband, Dr. Pierce, who had an affair with his wife's best friend."

"We'll call them the Ex and the Sex." Leatrice made a column for each on her pad of paper. "What's the evidence against each one?"

Kate tucked her feet under her. "Well, Dr. Harriman was arrested today for his ex-wife's murder."

"I'd say that's pretty strong evidence." Leatrice dropped the pad in her lap. "You think the police got the wrong person?"

"He'd been one of our top suspects, but he was arrested before someone tried to kill me today," I said. "If we go with the theory that the person who committed both of these murders is also out to get rid of me, then Dr. Harriman can't be the killer."

Leatrice picked up her paper again and gave my shoulder a pat. "Of course I believe you if you say someone tried to kill you, but let's look at the evidence against all the suspects before we eliminate anyone. No stone should go unturned."

"God forbid we skip a step in the private-investigator correspondence course," Kate muttered out of the corner of her mouth.

Leatrice ignored Kate. "So let's get back to the two husbands."

"First off, it had to be someone who knew she took blood-pressure medicine." I took the pillow from behind my head and sat up. "Both Dr. Harriman and Dr. Pierce fit the bill."

"We thought Dr. Harriman was the most likely killer," Kate said. "He attended the wedding and examined the body before the paramedics arrived. He also had an appointment with Mr. Boyd less than an hour before he died."

Leatrice kept her eyes on her notebook. "Motive and opportunity."

Kate sighed. "On the other hand, she treated Dr. Pierce horribly. He and Clara's best friend were having an affair and they won't waste any time now that she's gone. Also, they were both missing at the wedding when we found Clara, so they could have planned it together."

"A buddy system for murder." Leatrice tapped her pen on the legal pad.

"Don't forget what you found out about Helen Boyd, Annabelle." Kate sat forward and rested her elbows on her knees. Richard joined us from the kitchen, and I remembered that I'd been too dazed in the hospital to tell him my latest scoop.

"Mrs. Boyd knew all about her husband's affair with Mrs. Pierce. Mrs. Pierce wanted to blow the cover off the whole thing and destroy his career."

Richard drew his breath in sharply. "Why?"

"Because she could," I reminded him. "This is Mrs. Pierce we're talking about, after all. No loyalty. No forgiveness. Maybe Boyd did something to make her angry and she wanted to punish him. Who knows?"

"You're sure Mrs. Boyd knew?" Richard pressed.

I nodded. "The day before the wedding she showed up on Mrs. Pierce's doorstep threatening all sorts of things, including murder."

"I have a hard time imagining prim Mrs. Boyd making threats," Richard said.

Kate's eyes widened. "Where were you when she thought you killed her husband?"

"In a state of catatonic shock, I think." Richard put a hand on his forehead and swayed. "It's all fuzzy."

"She threatened to kill Mrs. Pierce," I assured them. "And called her every nasty word you can imagine."

"How marvelous." Richard smiled. "I bet I'd have thought of a few more choice words for her, though."

"Did anyone hear Mrs. Boyd say she'd kill your client?" Leatrice asked me.

"No, but Mrs. Pierce told Maxwell the whole story."

"Then it's hearsay." Leatrice made a note. "Not enough to build a case around."

"All this thinking has made my head pound." I picked up my purse to retrieve the pain medication the

182

hospital had given me. "Could you get me some water, Richard?"

He went into the kitchen, and I heard him searching for a clean glass. I opened my purse and took out the small box of wedding photos. "I almost forgot. The whole reason I went to see Maxwell Gray. The pictures from the Pierce wedding."

Kate took the box from me. "Are there any good shots of the Corcoran Gallery? We spent so much time designing the event."

I shrugged. "I didn't get a chance to look at them carefully."

"I wonder if we'll find anything in the pictures." Leatrice dropped her pad and pen and ran over to stand behind Kate.

"What are you hoping to find?" I asked.

"That concussion must have really affected you, dear," Leatrice looked up from the pictures. "I'm searching for clues to the murder."

I forgot all about my headache.

"Good thing these photos were in your purse or they'd be at the mechanic's with your car," Kate said.

My car had been hauled off to a Georgetown body shop in the hopes that my crumpled bumper and mangled grate could be repaired. I'd be without a car for at least a week. Not that I felt like driving anytime soon.

Leatrice thumbed through the first few photos. "What kind of wedding pictures are these? Who takes pictures of the food?"

Richard hurried from the kitchen and nudged

Leatrice to scoot over. "I asked Maxwell to get a few close-ups of the hors d'oeuvres and my displays. Let me see."

"The best way to find clues will be to find pictures of the victim." Leatrice instructed us. "See who she's with and who's near her. If we're lucky, we'll find some of our suspects lurking in the background."

"Have you ever seen such a spectacular blend of color on a sushi station?" Richard held up a picture. "The sweet sushi is a work of art. All my idea, naturally."

I handed Leatrice a print of Mrs. Pierce being escorted down the aisle by a handsome groomsman. "This is the victim. Clara Pierce."

"That's some hairdo." Leatrice studied the cotton candy helmet. Bold words coming from a woman in her eighties with jet black hair.

"I've got to hand it to Maxwell," Richard said. "He captured the true beauty of the chive-tied beggar's purse."

Leatrice strained to look at the photo in Richard's hand. "You serve food in a purse?"

Richard groaned and shook his head. "A beggar's purse is a term we use when we fill a crepe and tie it up into a tiny bundle. For these we used a long chive to make the bow on top. Have you ever seen anything so adorable?"

Leatrice took the picture from Richard. "Doesn't look like any purse I've ever owned."

Richard snatched the picture back and muttered

under his breath as he continued to admire it.

Kate passed a pile of prints to me. "There are lots of pictures with Clara, but most of them are portraits at the church."

"She looks fine in all of these," I said. "If she'd already been poisoned, it hadn't kicked in yet."

Leatrice held a photo an inch from her nose. "If I wanted to poison someone, I'd do it during a party where it's easier to slip it in food or drink. Not at a church."

"These are gorgeous table shots, Annabelle." Richard held up a square picture of one of the dining tables taken before the guests descended for dinner.

I took the picture from Richard and held it by the edges. Looking at the breathtaking flowers and coordinating Limoges china, I felt a twinge of regret. Each wedding had something go not quite right. Off-key soloist. Mediocre food. Late limousines. But not this wedding. We'd planned for a year so it would be perfect. It had been, except for the dead body.

"Check this out." Kate peered over Leatrice's shoulder. "The bride with Clara and Dr. Harriman."

"Neither parent looks happy," Leatrice said. "Good thing the daughter stood between them."

"I must get a copy of this one." Richard clapped his hands. "The caviar in the quail egg is like a tiny Fabergé masterpiece, if I do say so myself."

"Here's a classic." I lifted a photo of Clara and Bev Tripton out of the stack. They held each other around the waist and each had a drink in the other hand.

"They seem pretty chummy," Kate said.

Leatrice took the photo. "The victim's eyes are bloodshot. Maybe the poison had started to take effect."

"Here I am setting up the Indonesian satay station." Richard waved a photo in front of me. "Do you think that jacket makes me look hippy?"

I didn't bother to look. "No."

"I don't care for the way the side vents hang. I may have to cycle that suit out of the lineup."

"Another one of Mrs. Pierce with a drink in hand," I said.

"It appears to be the same drink, Annabelle." Leatrice pointed to the glass in Mrs. Pierce's hand. "See? Same type glass and same two little plastic straws."

"What?" Richard snapped his head up. "Hand me those pictures."

"Is there a problem?" Kate asked.

He jabbed at the photos. "You'd better believe there's a problem. These straws shouldn't be here."

"I'm not sure I follow you." I watched Richard stand up and take huge strides around the room, mumbling about straws. Maybe he'd finally lost it.

"I never use plastic straws at my parties. It would ruin the look of the entire event to have guests running around with tiny poles sticking out of their drinks."

"Curious." Leatrice took the two photos from Richard as he sank back onto the couch.

"I have no idea how those hideous things could

have landed on my bars."

"Do we have any pictures of the bars?" I asked. Kate and I sifted through the proofs, fanning them out on the coffee table.

"Right here." Kate held up a shot of a bar draped in white shimmery organza. The glasses were arranged in front with the bottles of liquor behind them. Small glasses of olives, onions, and lime wedges sat on both ends. No straws.

Richard inspected the photograph, and then tossed it back on the table. "Thank God. They didn't come from me."

Kate threw her hands in the air. "Then where did they come from?"

Leatrice slapped her knee. "I'll bet the murderer brought them. What better way to get poison into a drink?"

"If the poison was in powder form, the killer could have packed it into straws, dropped them in her drink, and let the poison dissolve," I said.

Kate leapt up. "Mrs. Pierce wouldn't think twice about it. Who'd notice a detail as insignificant as plastic straws but Richard?"

Richard appeared stuck somewhere between a smile and a frown.

"We've discovered how the murderer did it," I said. "Now we just have one tiny detail remaining."

"What's that?" Kate asked.

Leatrice let out her breath slowly. "Figure out which of the suspects is the murderer."

Chapter 27

"I think we should call the police in on this." Richard went into the kitchen and poured a glass of water. He remembered my headache. I took two pills out of the orange plastic cylinder then watched Richard drain the glass. Maybe not.

"Isn't the detective going to be upset with us?" Kate asked. "He told us not to go snooping around."

"We just stumbled across this clue." I stood up gingerly and walked to the kitchen. I took a Coke out of the refrigerator, then washed my pain medicine down with a big swallow. The caffeine and sugar would make me feel better, if nothing else.

"I'm not going to be the one who calls him," Kate shook her head. "Annabelle should call him. He likes her."

I shuffled back to the couch. "He does not."

"I'll bet you'd get a lot of sympathy, too." Kate mimicked a swoon. "All men love a damsel in a mess."

Richard cast his eyes around my apartment. "In this case, I think mess is the appropriate word."

"If I didn't have a concussion, I'd make you pay for saying that, Richard."

Leatrice picked up the phone and took a card out of her pocket. She dialed while she talked. "I'll call the detective. He's a nice young man. I'm sure he'll be happy to come over and get the evidence."

Come over? I didn't want him seeing me with a red knot in the middle of my forehead like a Cyclops. Couldn't someone drop it off at the station? I waved my arms to get her attention, but Leatrice was chatting away. She put the phone back on its charger.

"Detective Reese is more than happy to come right over and hear about our evidence. He's especially interested in your accident."

"How does he know about that?" I could hear my voice getting shrill. "I didn't hear you tell him."

"News travels fast when you have a police radio."

I couldn't jaywalk without this guy finding out. I got up and headed down the hall to the bathroom, walking lightly on my sore knee. At least I could find some makeup to cover my bump and maybe brush my hair.

"Where are you going?" Richard called after me. "You're the star attraction."

"This star needs to freshen up. I feel disgusting after being in the hospital all afternoon."

"Do you want some help with your makeup?" Kate followed me to the bathroom door. "If we give you full, pouty lips, the emphasis will be off your forehead."

They'd have to be enormous lips for anyone not to notice the lump on my head. "Thanks, but I'm not going to fix myself up for Reese. I just want to wash my face."

"Suit yourself."

I closed the door and rummaged through the contents of the vanity drawers. Powder, mascara, and lipstick were usually the extent of my makeup routine. I knew

I had some old liquid foundation in here somewhere, though. I pulled out a handful of perfume samples in their small, paper folders. The plastic stoppers had loosened on a couple and the contents of the vials spilled onto my hands. I choked at the combination of the spicy musk and tea rose scents.

I jammed my hand into the back of the last drawer and found a tube of brown cream concealer. A bit of hard makeup snaked out as I squeezed the tube. It would have to do. I dabbed it on my knot and flinched. Still sore. I patted the brown over the surface of the bump until it looked like a beige lump instead of a red one. Good enough.

"I feel much better." I walked out of the bathroom and down the hall.

Kate saw me, and her eyes bulged. "What did you do to your head?"

"Is it too obvious?"

Richard came out of the kitchen and held his nose. "Who's going to notice her head with that awful smell?"

My eyes started to tear. I felt as horrible as I must have looked. "I spilled some perfume on my hands."

"Some?" Richard backed away from me.

Leatrice came and put her arm around me. She scowled at Richard and Kate. "You've had a frightful day. No one expects you to look perfect after being in a car accident. If anyone understands that, Detective Reese will."

I let her lead me to the sofa and put cushions under

my head and feet. "I didn't do it for Detective Reese, Leatrice."

"Of course not, dear. I'm sure he won't notice a thing." Leatrice left me, and I could hear her in the hallway scolding Kate and Richard in hushed tones. After a few minutes, she went to the door. "I hear footsteps."

No doubt her superhuman hearing had been developed over years of eavesdropping.

Mrs. Butters flung open the door, but her smile evaporated when she saw Alexandra and not Detective Reese. She gave Alexandra's pink crop pants and pink-and-green plaid purse the once-over. "Who are you?"

"I'm Alexandra." She held out a white box. "I brought some sweets for the injured."

"Come on in," I called out from the couch. "How did you find out so fast?"

Alexandra pointed in Kate's direction.

I raised an eyebrow at Kate. "I don't think you've ever been this efficient."

Kate shrugged. "I made some calls from the hospital. So shoot me."

Alexandra placed the box in front of me. "I brought you samples of your favorite cake flavors."

I rubbed my hands together. "The dark chocolate truffle and the lemon curd?"

She nodded and sat next to me. "Are these pictures from the Pierce wedding?"

Richard ran up and joined us on the couch. "Wait until you see the food shots. To die for!"

"Are there any of the cake?" Alexandra pawed through the photos. She held up a photo of Mr. and Mrs. Pierce. "Who is this man looking so chummy with Mrs. Pierce?"

Kate's eyes widened. "What do you mean? That's her husband. You saw them arguing, remember?"

Alexandra shook her head. "That's not who I saw her fighting with."

My jaw hit the floor. "Who did you see her fighting with then?"

"What's all this about?" Leatrice couldn't contain the curiosity in her voice.

"Alexandra told the police that she saw Mr. and Mrs. Pierce fighting before the wedding, but it seems like it wasn't Mr. Pierce after all."

Alexandra sifted through the stack and held up a photo of the bride with her father. Dr. Harriman. "This is the one."

I exchanged glances with Kate. "Are you sure?" It looked more and more as if the police arrested the right person. The bump on my head made me think otherwise, though.

"Of course." Alexandra looked taken aback. "This one is much better looking than her husband."

"She's right," Kate said. "You could never say that Dr. Pierce is as distinguished as Dr. Harriman."

Richard took the photo from Alexandra. "I have to admit, his silver hair is quite striking."

I threw my hands in the air. "This is a murder investigation, not a beauty contest."

"I'm surprised to hear you're still investigating the murders." Detective Reese stepped inside the open door, nodding at Kate and at Richard, who shrank back against the wall. Alexandra brightened at the sight of the detective and didn't notice Leatrice glaring at her.

I had to admit that in his black jeans and leather jacket, Reese looked a bit menacing. In a sexy way. The detective took a seat across the coffee table from me.

"I didn't mean investigation," I stammered.

He nodded, then changed the subject. "I hear you were a victim of road rage this afternoon."

"Is that what they called it in the police report?"

"I didn't see a police report. You weren't hit in my district," Reese said. "I have friends in the Virginia office, though."

"You were checking up on me?" I exchanged looks with Kate.

"Miss Archer, I'm a detective." Reese raised an eyebrow. "Checking up on people involved in my cases falls into the job description."

I felt a flush creeping up my neck. "Well, it wasn't a case of road rage, Detective."

"What would you call it?"

I touched a hand to my head. "Attempted murder sounds more accurate."

Reese laughed. "Just because you were a victim of a hit-and-run doesn't mean the driver tried to kill you. These kinds of things happen all the time."

"The car didn't just bump into me and drive away." I

swung my feet down. "He rammed me twice and pushed me off the road."

Reese swept a hand through his hair. "Are you sure you aren't exaggerating?"

"Do you think I got a concussion from being tapped on the bumper, Detective?" I pointed to my lump. "It looked even worse a few hours ago."

"I don't see how." Reese stared at my forehead, a puzzled expression on his face. "Maybe you should consider airbags."

"Thanks for the tip." It would be much easier to dislike him, I thought, if he weren't so good-looking.

"I find it hard to believe that someone would want to kill you." Reese locked eyes with me. "Murder is serious business."

I threw up my hands. "I'm glad you noticed."

"We think the killer tried to get rid of Annabelle because she knows too much," Kate insisted.

"That's impossible. We arrested Dr. Harriman this afternoon for the murder of Clara Pierce. That was before your accident."

I crossed my arms over my chest. "We heard. Maybe he had an accomplice, though."

"You think you know something the entire police department doesn't?" Reese cast a look at all of us. Richard shook his head vigorously, and Alexandra just smiled.

"We know that Mrs. Boyd threatened to kill Mrs. Pierce the day before the wedding," Kate said. "Maybe she was in on it with Dr. Harriman."

"Please don't tell me how you got this information." Reese gave a weary glance in my direction.

"It just fell in our laps." I shrugged my shoulders.

"I'll bet it did." Reese stood. "I appreciate the call, but I can't run around chasing rumors. I need hard evidence."

Leatrice rushed to his side. "That's why we called you. We do have evidence. We figured out how the murderer administered the poison."

"Go on." Reese sat back down. "I'm listening."

"Take a look at these photos." Leatrice handed him the pictures of Mrs. Pierce holding her cocktail. "Do you see anything out of place?"

He studied them for a moment. "No."

"Exactly." Leatrice danced around him. "The normal person wouldn't think twice when seeing these."

"Luckily, Richard isn't normal," I said. Payback for his comment about my messy apartment.

Leatrice pointed to the photographs. "These aren't Richard's straws. He doesn't use them, and they weren't on the bars. We checked."

"Are you sure?" Reese sounded interested.

Richard peered down his nose at Reese. "Of course I'm sure. I'd die before using a cocktail straw for a wedding."

"Clara is the only one with a straw in her drink." Kate handed him a handful of reception shots. "See for yourself."

"So you came to the conclusion that the straw held the poison?" The corner of the detective's mouth twitched into a grin. "Not bad deductive reasoning."

"You think we're right?" Leatrice's bell necklace jingled as she bounced up and down on her toes.

"I can't say for sure, but it makes sense to me. Do you mind if I take these pictures back to the station?"

"Could you leave the ones of the hors d'oeuvres? The shot of the caviar-filled quail egg should go in a frame." Richard started weeding through the prints spread out on the coffee table, then stopped when he saw Reese's face. "Or you could take them all and bring them back whenever you're done."

"Just because you found this clue, doesn't mean I want you hunting for others." Reese directed his comments to me. "We've got the murderer locked up, remember?"

"You're sure Dr. Harriman did it?" Kate asked.

"He had motive and opportunity for both murders, and now we might know the way he killed Mrs. Pierce." Reese held up the photos.

"And I saw him arguing with Mrs. Pierce at the wedding," Alexandra said, giving Reese a look that was either sheepish or flirtatious. "I got the husbands switched at first, but now I'm sure it was Dr. Harriman."

"What about Mrs. Boyd?" Kate didn't sound convinced. "We just forget about her?"

"Just because someone threatens murder, doesn't mean they did it." Reese met my eyes. "I don't want to hear about any more snooping around from any of you."

I gave him a sugary smile. "I'm going to be taking it easy for a while. You don't have to hit me over the head for me to get the hint."

His eyes flitted to my poorly concealed bump. "At least not twice, I hope."

Chapter 28

"I'm telling you, Annabelle. Maxwell sounded upset that you took the proofs." Kate stood outside the bathroom and spoke through the door. We'd survived the night together, but we were having a hard time negotiating time in the one bathroom.

"You talked to him?"

"While you were in the shower just now. He said he left a couple of messages yesterday, too."

"Did you tell him that I got run off the road and had to be taken to the hospital?" I dried off and put on my plush Willard Hotel bathrobe, last year's Christmas gift from their catering department. "Otherwise I'd have returned them right away."

"I tried, but he kept talking about how upset the clients were when they couldn't see the photos. Should I call the bride and explain that we gave them to the police?"

"Don't bother." Not likely to do any good, anyway. A bride would cut you slack only if you produced a death certificate. "I'll be out in a couple of minutes and I'll deal with it."

I wrapped a smoke-blue towel around my hair like a turban, trying not to make it too tight. The shower had washed off the last bits of makeup and the knot on my head shone like a shiny new penny. Maybe I'd let Kate have a go at downplaying it with pouty lips.

"Thanks for taking this morning's phone calls." I passed the office on the way to my bedroom.

Kate had the phone pressed to her ear and she rolled her eyes, mouthing the words "Alice Freakmont." Mrs. Pierce's death had elevated Alice Freemont to the role of our most demanding client. We called her Freakmont because she called at least once a day to freak out about something.

"What is it this time?" I whispered.

Kate covered the mouthpiece with her hand. "Is it okay for her bridal attendants to go bare-legged in July?"

"Tell her the latest trend is for bridesmaids to wear nothing at all under their gowns."

Kate held the phone at arm's length while she laughed. Just the thought of Alice, arguably the biggest priss on the planet, telling her bridesmaids to go naked under their formal, A-line dresses made me feel better.

I continued into my bedroom and stepped out of my robe. I pulled on a white fitted T-shirt with my favorite jeans and did a deep knee bend to stretch out the seat. A little tight but wearable. I had to stop letting Richard cook. He didn't know how to make anything with less than a stick of butter.

"Yoo-hoo, anyone home?" Speak of the devil.

I stuck my head into the hallway and saw Richard coming toward me in a navy suit. "We're conservative today, aren't we?"

He opened the jacket and flashed the melon-orange lining. "Fooled you. This is my mood-swing suit." Kate stepped out of the office. "Just what you need."

Richard buttoned the jacket back up. "What are we up to today, ladies?"

"I have big plans to do nothing," I said. "I'm still recuperating from yesterday, and I promised Reese I would stay out of trouble."

"You were serious about that?" Richard followed me into the kitchen. "The other times you promised to stop snooping around you never did."

"But now we have the clue that proves how the murderer poisoned Mrs. Pierce," I said.

"So now you don't care about finding out who killed her?"

"You heard the detective," I insisted. "They caught the killer."

"But you aren't totally convinced, are you?" Richard gave me a suspicious look. I could tell he didn't trust me not to run off and try to solve the murder.

"My gut tells me the killer is still on the loose," I shrugged. "If you have any bright ideas how to figure out who it is without making my head pound, I'm all ears."

"We've talked to everyone involved in the case." Kate squeezed by me and leaned against the counter. "How much more will we really be able to find out?"

"We're the only ones who think the murderer is still at large." Richard shook his head. "Maybe we're wrong."

"To be honest, we can't afford to spend any more time running around looking for clues." I poured myself a cup of lukewarm coffee. "Kate and I have another wedding this weekend, which we've hardly had time to think about."

"Luckily the bride and groom are laid back and the whole thing has been planned for months," Kate said. "I talked to them this morning. The rehearsal is still set for six o'clock tonight."

I smacked myself on the head, then instantly regretted it. "I forgot about the rehearsal."

"Don't worry about it, Annabelle." Kate waved her hand. "I'm going to run it for you. You're not in any shape to deal with rowdy groomsmen at this point."

"Thanks. You're right." I sighed. "But I feel like there's something else I've forgotten about. Something important."

Richard cleared his throat and pointed over the counter to the pile of plastic tuxedo bags stacked on the arm of the couch. "They've been sitting here for almost a week. Are you planning on keeping them?"

I cringed. "That's what I forgot to do. Return the tuxedos from the Pierce wedding. The fines will be more than the cost to rent them in the first place."

"Maybe if you explain the whole story, the guy at the tuxedo shop will give you a break," Kate said. "Don't you know him pretty well?"

"Yes, and after all the weddings I've sent him, he should let me have the tuxedos outright."

"Do you want to go now and return them? I'll take you." Richard, sounding eager to have a mission, went to gather up the garment bags. "I don't have anything to do since I'm still under police orders not to work."

"Should you be going out so soon, Annabelle?" Kate asked.

I put my cup in the sink. "I'll be fine."

"Okay, I'll hold down the fork while you're gone."

Richard opened the door and let me pass. A smirk curled the side of his mouth. "Now that I'd like to see."

Chapter 29

"Sauro's is two blocks down on the left." We exited Dupont Circle onto Nineteenth Street and drove past a series of formal restaurants catering to business executives. Waiters were sweeping off the sidewalks in front. Warm enough to eat outside if you could handle the exhaust fumes.

"I'll drop you off, then circle the block for street parking."

I'd have been finished before he found a space. Not the easiest place in the world to park. "Why don't you park in one of the garages?"

"No, thank you. The last time I let a parking attendant have my car he readjusted the seats, reprogrammed my radio, and jammed my roof open."

"That's right. I remember it rained that day."

"Exactly." Richard pressed his lips together as he pulled over. "I looked like an absolute fool driving around in a convertible holding an umbrella."

"Fair enough." I stepped out onto the curb, dragging the garment bags behind me. "I'll be waiting."

I pushed the glass door to Sauro Custom Tailor open with my hip. Mr. Sauro appeared from the back of the shop and took the bags from me, laying them out across the counter.

"Another successful wedding?" He flashed me a smile as he thumbed through the bags, moving his lips as he counted. Mr. Sauro looked the same as he always did, a tape measure around his neck and silvery hair showing traces of once being dark. His hands were worn from hemming and tucking thousands of suits over the years. I wondered how many grooms he'd seen come through his store.

"You could say that," I said. Most people who knew Mrs. Pierce would call it a great success.

"Almost a week late." He gave a low whistle, and then winked at me. "Don't worry about it."

"Thanks, Mr. Sauro. I promise it won't happen again."

He waved off my apologies and opened the top bag. "Let me check the pockets. Don't want to end up with an extra wallet."

"I haven't even opened the bags, so I hope all the components are there." I sat down on the step stool in front of the wall-length mirrors and watched Mr. Sauro hang the suits on a metal bar as he inspected them.

"When will we see your groom in here picking out his wedding clothes?"

"Not for a while." I felt myself blush. "I'm too busy with work right now to think about marriage."

Mr. Sauro made clucking noises. "I have a feeling the right man will walk into your life soon."

Richard swung open the glass door and stumbled into the shop. "The best spot I could find is two blocks away in an alley. I'm starting to perspire."

"Well, we're almost finished here." I stood up so Richard could sit on the stool.

"Take your time. I'm not going back out there until I cool down." Richard took off his jacket and fanned himself with a brochure for After Six formalwear. "One drop of sweat and this shirt will be ruined."

"A cigarette lighter and an empty plastic baggy." Mr. Sauro held up the two items. "That's all I found in the pockets."

I took both from him as he went into the back of the store. I rolled the thin, silver lighter in my palm. Not the cheap, drugstore variety. I would need to call around and try to find its owner. I began to wad up the plastic bag when some white powder fell out onto my hand. I opened the bag and shook it, causing a small pile of white to gather in the pointy corner.

"Richard, take a look at this."

"You've never seen a sandwich bag before?" Richard held his shirt away from his body with his fingertips.

"Not one with white stuff like this in it. Besides, why

would one of the men have a sandwich baggy in his pocket?"

Richard walked over and took the bag from me "Well, what do you think it is?"

"I think it's poison."

Richard shrieked as though he'd been burned and dropped the bag to the floor. "How could you let me touch it? I've been contaminated. Where's a sink? I need to get this off my hands."

"Not that kind of poison," I said. "The blood-pressure medication that caused Mrs. Pierce to die."

Richard reached down and retrieved the bag, holding it away from him by the edges. "So whoever killed her carried the straws around in this bag, waiting for the right time to drop them in her drink?"

"It makes sense, doesn't it? If only we could determine whose tuxedo this came from, but they're all alike."

"Were Dr. Pierce's and Dr. Harriman's tuxedos both in the pile we returned?" Richard ran a fingertip along the row of hanging black jackets.

I nodded. "The bride wanted all the men to match so she asked her father and stepfather to rent the same style as the groom and groomsmen. I counted eight tuxedos total, so they're all here. It could have been either of them."

Richard jerked his hand away from the tuxedos. "Think about it, Annabelle. The murderer's clothes have been sitting in your apartment all week, and we didn't even know it."

Chapter 30

"The question is, does the murderer know I've been sitting on this evidence?" I carried Richard's suit jacket in one hand and the plastic baggy in the other. He walked in front of me, taking up most of the sidewalk by holding his arms out so they wouldn't touch his body.

"That would explain why you've been a target."

"It didn't even occur to me that the killer's clothes were in that pile of tuxedos. Now I understand why someone broke into my apartment."

"Why did he put his tuxedo in with the others to be returned if he didn't want anyone to find the evidence?"

"Maybe he forgot about the baggy in all the commotion following the murder." We rounded the corner into a narrow alley where Richard's car sat between two TOW AWAY ZONE signs. A white slip of paper peeked from underneath his windshield wiper. "There's no such thing as the perfect crime."

Richard took the parking ticket from the windshield and folded it without looking inside. "Don't they say that when a murder is committed the killer makes a hundred mistakes?"

"Something like that." I opened the passenger door. "Aren't you going to look at the ticket?"

"It's a fake. I always put that out when I park illegally."

"I wouldn't suggest using it when we park at the police station."

"You're serious about going there now, Annabelle?"

"We should give this evidence to Reese as soon as possible." I lowered myself into the leather seat. "I'm not crazy about the idea of hanging on to it any longer than I already have."

"But isn't this more evidence against Dr. Harriman, the person we don't think did it?"

I shrugged. "I guess so, but it could've been Dr. Pierce just as easily."

"Or any one of the groomsmen."

"Why would the groomsmen want to kill the bride's mother?" I raised an eyebrow. "They didn't even know her."

"Just a thought," Richard mumbled. "They did meet her, after all. After I met Mrs. Pierce the first time, I wanted to kill her."

I rubbed my temples. "Just drive."

"I'm warning you." Richard eased the car out of the alley and edged his way into traffic. "The District Two police station isn't glamorous, and it certainly isn't clean."

"We won't stay long. I'll just hand this over and leave. I don't want to take up time the police could be using to build their case."

"So now you're admitting that Dr. Harriman might be the killer?" Richard drove around Dupont Circle and headed down Massachusetts Avenue, passing embassy after embassy.

"Finding the traces of poison in the tuxedo rules out our female suspects. Mrs. Boyd may have threatened to kill Mrs. Pierce, and Bev may have wanted her beloved best friend out of the way, but a man carried the poison straws in his pocket."

"Such a shame, too. Helen Boyd would have made a spectacular Lady Macbeth."

"The killer also had to know which medicine Mrs. Pierce took, which drug would kill her when mixed with her medication, and have easy access to prescription drugs."

Richard went around another traffic circle without slowing. "Which both Harriman and Pierce did, since they'd both lived with her and they're both doctors."

"But of the two, only Harriman had access to Mr. Boyd before the tasting, so he could have killed both victims."

"Which means that someone else tried to run you off the road."

"Maybe he sent his new wife to deal with me once he was arrested. But he seemed so pleasant when Kate and I talked to him at the bride's house."

Richard drummed his fingers on the steering wheel. "A real Dr. Jekyll and Mr. Hyde. How did he know you'd have the tuxedos, though?"

"I announced to all the men in the wedding that they should leave their formalwear with the coat check at the end of the night and I'd return them. He must have forgotten all about the baggy when he dropped off his tuxedo."

"Probably too excited about Mrs. Pierce's death." Richard sped through a yellow light to cross Wisconsin Avenue, and then veered off into a neighborhood with alternating colonial and Cape Cod-style houses. After several blocks, he slowed and parallel parked beside a low brick building with several police cruisers in the adjoining lot. Grass covered the front lawn of the building, and a web of tree branches provided shade for the cars. Not how I'd imagined an urban police station.

"This isn't so bad, Richard." I stepped out of the car and crossed the street. I didn't see the bustle of police officers and shady characters I'd expected. It looked almost deserted. "From the way you described it, I thought there would be convicts in leg shackles being dragged away for floggings."

"Where did you get that absurd idea?" Richard strolled across the street buttoning his jacket. "I stand by my assessment of the bathrooms, though."

We walked up the sidewalk to the glass double doors. As Richard reached for the metal push bars, both doors flew open. A group of officers rushed past us. Richard stumbled backward onto the pavement, and I tripped over him, landing cleanly in his lap.

"I don't believe it."

I gazed up at the source of the deep, mocking voice. Reese. Who else? I tried to push myself off of Richard, who made high-pitched gasping noises. Reese pulled me up by one hand with such strength that I bumped against his chest. I'd never been so close to him before. I backed away and felt my cheeks flush.

"We were looking for you, Detective. We wanted to give you this." I held out the plastic baggy.

Reese took the bag and cocked an eyebrow. "Thanks. I can never get too many of these."

"For heaven's sake, Annabelle." Richard stood up and flicked specks of dirt off his hands. "Stop blushing like a schoolgirl and explain what it is."

I shot daggers at Richard. "We found it in the pocket of one of the wedding tuxedos. We think the killer used it to carry the straws filled with poison."

"See the white powder in the bottom?" Richard poked at the bag with his pinkie finger.

Reese held the bag up. "Whose tux did it come from?"

"That's where things get confusing." Richard twisted to dust off the seat of his pants. "Annabelle collected all the tuxedos from the wedding party and the fathers. They've been sitting in her apartment since Monday night, waiting to be returned."

"After the burglary," Reese said.

Richard took a step toward Reese. "We think the killer remembered the evidence in his jacket and came looking for it. But we hadn't yet brought them in from my car, so he didn't find anything."

"Did they all realize that you would have the tuxedos, Annabelle?"

"I told all the men who were part of the wedding that I'd take their clothes back to the shop for them."

"Pretty nice of you." Reese gave me a half grin. "Do you do that for all weddings?"

I returned his smile. "I told you I'm full service."

"Does the bag help at all, Detective?" Richard took off his jacket. I noticed Reese's eyes pause on the orange lining.

"I'll have the lab run some tests on it. I have a feeling you're right about this powder. Combined with the evidence we have from Boyd's murder, this should lock Dr. Harriman away for a long time."

"You determined that he killed Boyd, too?" Richard hooked his jacket on his finger and swung it over his shoulder.

"Mr. Boyd died from an overdose of a cardiovascular drug, not poisoned soup. We found the needle mark." Reese gave Richard a quick nod. "You're off the hook."

Richard gave an exaggerated sigh of relief. "Free at last." You'd have thought he'd been locked in solitary confinement for a month.

"That explains everything but my accident." I looked between Richard and Reese. "We still have to figure out who tried to kill me."

"I don't think you have anything to worry about, Annabelle." Reese squeezed my arm. "You can hang up your detective badge. Our case against Dr. Harriman is airtight."

Chapter 31

"That's what he said?" Kate sat on the floor of my office packing small Tiffany boxes into shopping bags.

"I guess they have enough proof to link him to both." I sat down in my office chair. The blue boxes had taken up my entire floor for two weeks, and I was glad to see them go.

"I should have known from when he failed the cleavage test."

"Kate, if we relied on your method of testing suspects, half the city would be in jail now, including most of the police force."

"He still doesn't seem the type to commit cold-blooded murder. He sounded genuinely concerned about his daughter that day we visited her."

I shook my head. "You never can tell about people."

"I'm a little sorry the whole thing's over."

"That's because your life wasn't in danger." I used a fat Magic Marker to cross off several days on the wall-size calendar above my desk. I'd been so preoccupied with the murder case, I'd fallen behind almost an entire week. "It may have been exciting, but I'll be glad for things to get back to normal."

"I guess we can close the books on the Pierce wedding now."

"The only thing left is to attend the memorial service tomorrow morning."

"You must be joking!" Kate dropped a handful of favor boxes, and I heard the sound of tinkling glass. I hoped we had extras.

"I think it would be nice of us to pay our respects to the bride. We liked her, remember?"

The corners of Kate's mouth turned down. "I didn't like her that much."

"We'll sit in the back and sneak out as soon as it's over. You have to go with me," I begged.

"Why can't Richard take you?" Kate whined.

"He's going to meet us at the church. He'll be coming straight from a meeting."

"But I have to prepare for our wedding," Kate argued. "I don't have time."

"The funeral is at ten a.m. and the wedding isn't until six o'clock. Do you have any other excuses you want to try out?"

"Give me a second. I'm sure I can come up with one."

I tapped my foot. "I'm waiting."

"You're still recovering from your accident. Too much exertion could be bad for you."

"How much could I exert myself at a memorial service?"

"I don't know. You saw the party Bev had in her honor." Kate wagged her finger at me in warning. "If she's in charge, there could be conga lines and limbo contests."

"No harm ever came from going to a funeral, Kate. The murderer is behind bars, so we're all safe. There's nothing to worry about."

Kate let out a breath. "You keep saying that."

Chapter 32

Leatrice knelt next to the tiny flower bed in front of our building and jumped up when I walked out the door. She wore a long denim apron with rows of pockets, each with a gardening tool or a different type of seed packet peeking out the top. I fantasized about getting one for weddings, so I could keep my emergency supplies with me at all times. With brides, you never knew when you'd need superglue, safety pins, or aspirin. The aspirin was more for me.

"Doing some morning gardening, Leatrice?" I held the door open for Kate, who carried two over-sized shopping bags full of favors for the evening's wedding.

"Best time to be outside." Leatrice tugged her apron straight. "Where are you two going so early? I rarely see you up and about before eleven."

"We're going to Mrs. Pierce's funeral." Kate shuffled a few steps down the walk. "Aren't you jealous?"

I knew Kate meant it sarcastically, but I could see that Leatrice didn't. I could just imagine us walking into the church with Leatrice trailing behind in her apron and green-and-pink-flowered gardening hat.

"You won't be missing much, Leatrice," I said. "The case is closed."

"I heard last night."

"How did you find out, Leatrice?" Kate glanced at me and raised an eyebrow.

"The eleven o'clock news. They showed your detective friend making a statement."

I needed to start paying more attention to current events. First I'd missed the leak in the newspaper, and now I'd missed seeing Reese on the news. I wondered if he wore a uniform or if he always wore street clothes on the job.

"It turns out that Mrs. Pierce's ex-husband killed her and Mr. Boyd." Kate rested the bulging bags on the sidewalk.

"Did the evidence we found help at all?" Leatrice asked. "Do you think they'll call on us to be witnesses at the trial?"

I could just imagine Leatrice taking the stand in the rhinestone tiara she wore for special occasions.

I suppressed a smile. "They have enough physical evidence and probably won't need our testimony."

Leatrice looked deflated, and I patted her on the arm. "I'm sure that Detective Reese won't hesitate to call you if he needs a reliable witness."

"Too bad he won't be coming around any more." Leatrice reached into one of her many pockets for a tissue and dabbed at her nose.

"Don't take it too hard." Kate took a few steps to her car and unlocked the trunk.

Leatrice sniffled and stuffed the tissue back in her apron. "Allergies. It must be all the pollen."

"I'm sure you'll see Reese again." Kate packed the

shopping bags into the trunk and slammed it shut. "Annabelle can't seem to stay out of trouble."

"That's true," Leatrice smiled.

I slid into the passenger seat next to Kate. "Sorry Leatrice, we have to hurry if we're going to make it to the funeral on time."

"Sometimes I think she's got hats in the belfry," Kate said as she jerked the car in gear and pulled away from the sidewalk. I started to correct her, then just rolled my eyes and took my cell phone out of my purse.

"I'm going to call Richard and make sure he's on his way."

"Don't worry. We'll know plenty of people at the funeral."

I held the phone to my ear. "Most of them were on our suspect list at one point, remember?"

Kate gripped the steering wheel with both hands. "They don't serve communion wine at funerals, do they?"

"We're not going to be poisoned, if that's what you're thinking," I assured her. "Dr. Harriman is behind bars."

"With this bunch, I'm not going to take any chances." Kate pressed her lips together.

Richard finally answered his phone. "Annabelle, is that you?"

"We should be at the church in a few minutes. Where are you?"

"I've been a bit delayed. I'll try to get there as soon as possible."

"Is anything wrong?"

"All I have to say is that Neiman Marcus shouldn't send invitations to a secret sale if they intend to open it up to everyone and their brother. I might as well be at Filene's Basement."

"That's your important meeting? A sale at Neiman's?"

Kate's mouth fell open. "He'd better be joking."

"This isn't just any old sale, darling. Prada is half price and not last year's line, either." I heard lots of voices in the background. "Oh, dear. I'm being jostled in the checkout line. Do you people have no concept of personal space?"

I assumed he wasn't talking to me. "I didn't think you shopped like the rest of us mortals."

"My Neiman's personal shopper is out sick, if you can believe the rotten luck. Don't worry about me, though. Listen, I've got to run. They're opening a new counter." The line went dead.

Kate narrowed her eyes. "Tell me he's coming."

"Well, the good news is he's next in line."

The sharp asymmetrical spires of National Presbyterian Church jutted into the sky in front of us. Not exactly your typical white clapboard church with a cross on top. We parked in the huge paved lot, but neither of us made a move to open our doors.

"I'm not going in," Kate said. "There's hardly anybody here yet."

Only a few other cars were in the lot with us, mostly European imports. The university stickers in the back windows of the cars read like a Who's Who of colleges. Princeton, Columbia, Duke, Harvard, Yale.

"Get down." I slid down below the dashboard. "Dr. and Mrs. Donovan just pulled up."

"The bride and groom?" Kate ducked behind the steering wheel. "I thought we were here to see the bride. Why are we hiding?"

"See her, yes. But I don't want to have a long conversation with her. She's probably still upset about the pictures." I peeked over the dash. Dr. Donovan drove the navy blue Mercedes into a space across from us. I noticed the stickers on his back windshield. Andover, Princeton, Harvard. His car must feel right at home.

"Elizabeth doesn't look so good," Kate whispered as the bride walked into the church on her husband's arm. "How could she get more frail and delicate?"

"Don't forget, her mother's dead and her father was arrested for the murder."

"Poor girl. She doesn't have anyone left except her husband." Kate pressed her brows together, and a tiny crease formed between her eyes. "But if I had to be left with one person, I wouldn't mind it being him. He's at least a nine."

I groaned. "I'm not sure which is more tasteless, rating the groom or doing it at a funeral."

"Give me a break. This is no normal funeral." Kate sat back up halfway when the bride and groom disappeared inside the building. "Have you ever seen such cheery people in your life?"

Cars were coming in a steady stream by then,

depositing black-clad mourners with big smiles on their faces. Couples greeted each other with air kisses and pats on the back.

"Just be thankful there aren't mimes this time," I said.

Just then a sharp rap came on my window. "Problem, ladies?"

Chapter 33

I raised my head and saw Fern standing next to the car door. He wore a long black jacket that reached down to his knees and a frilly white shirt that puffed up around his neck.

"What are you doing down there, girls?"

"You scared me to death." I pulled myself up from the floor of the car and opened the door. "I thought you were somebody else."

"You were waiting for someone hunched up on the floor of the car?"

"No. It's just that each time I'm doing something strange the same person seems to catch me." I stood up and brushed off my dress.

Kate came around the car to stand beside me. "A cute detective, no less."

"Tell me about this detective." Fern put an arm around Kate and his eyes widened with excitement. "How cute?"

"What you might call tall, dark, and ruggedly handsome," Kate said.

"Good." He fluffed the ruffles on his shirt. "I don't like pretty boys."

"He's not too tall." I avoided Kate's eyes. "And nothing went on between us, Fern, so you can wipe that grin off your face."

Kate put her foot up on the bumper of the car and straightened her stocking. "She's playing hard to get."

"I'm surprised you've heard of it." Fern arched his eyebrow as he appraised Kate's hemline.

"I didn't say I endorse it," Kate laughed. Somehow Fern could get away with saying outrageous things to just about anyone and make them love him for it.

He winked at me. "Let's not forget why we're here, girls."

I nodded solemnly. "You're right. We're here to pay our respects."

"Wrong." Fern lowered his voice as a group of women passed us. "We're here to critique what all these society tramps are wearing."

I looked around to see if anyone had heard him. "Half of them are your clients," I said in shock.

"Don't worry," he reassured me with a grin. "I call them tramps to their faces."

I believed him.

Kate linked her arms with ours. "This funeral might not be so bad after all."

Fern led us up the sidewalk and into the side door of the church. We walked down a hallway lined with large floral arrangements. Tall, spiky gladiolas seemed to be the flower of the day, with white lilies coming in a close second.

Fern made a face. "I can never look at a gladiola without thinking of death."

"We should have sent a huge bouquet of birds-of-paradise," Kate said. "That would be different."

"Do you notice anything odd?" I pulled Fern and Kate close to me. "They used the same color scheme as the wedding. All creams and whites with hints of blush."

Fern shivered and rubbed his arms. "You gave me the chills, Annabelle."

"Too bad it's been a week since the wedding or they could have reused the same flowers," Kate added.

"Why not?" Fern smoothed the front of his jacket. "I had to fix Clara's hair the same way she wore it at the wedding."

I winced. "I forgot about that. How awful, working on Mrs. Pierce."

Fern shrugged. "For once, the tramp couldn't talk back."

I stifled a laugh and thought that if I listened hard, I might hear Clara trying to do just that. We hung back as most of the crowd thinned out and went inside the main sanctuary. Elizabeth and her husband greeted people at the entrance, the doctor clearly holding his wife up. Her vacant expression and glassy eyes didn't leave much doubt she'd taken sedatives to get through the service.

"Do you recognize anyone?" Kate tried to hide behind a large fan-shaped spray of flowers.

"There's Bev Tripton." I joined Kate behind the arrangement as Bev entered the hallway. "Can you believe the outfit?"

Mrs. Pierce's devoted best friend wore a black suit with a wide portrait neckline, her ample cleavage protruding. The netting that extended from her black pillbox hat covered her face and came to rest on the exposed part of her breasts.

Kate did a double take. "Well, at least it's black."

"Who is she kidding with the veil?" Fern made clicking noises with his tongue. "And that hat is all wrong for her face."

"Here comes Dr. Pierce," I whispered to Fern through a palm frond. "I'll bet they came together and just walked in separately so it wouldn't look bad."

"This is ridiculous." Fern moved the greenery away from my face. "It looks like I'm talking to a floral arrangement with four legs."

I stepped out from behind the flowers. "I guess you could say we're having a hard time getting out of sleuth mode."

"Do you plan to spend all day out here, girls, or can we go inside?" Fern prodded us forward. We'd only advanced a few feet when loud footsteps approached from behind. I glanced over my shoulder and saw Helen Boyd striding toward the chapel in a fire-engine-red dress. I turned around so she wouldn't recognize me.

"Talk about tramp." Fern's jaw dropped open as Mrs. Boyd passed us. "Who is that?"

"Remember the man you told us that Mrs. Pierce had an affair with?" I said. "That's his wife."

Fern slapped a hand to his cheek. "This is going to be the best social event of the entire year. Hurry!"

As we reached the door of the chapel, my cell phone began singing. I never remembered to set it on silent mode. I flipped it open and cupped my hand around the mouthpiece.

"I'm on my way, Annabelle." Richard's voice echoed as if he were in a well.

"Hold on a second," I said to Fern and Kate, and then ran outside to get better reception. The closer I walked toward the parking lot, the clearer Richard sounded.

"Has the service started yet?"

"No, but we were just about to sit down. How far away are you?"

Richard's voice faded in and out. "I'm on the parkway, not quite at the CIA."

"I thought you were at Neiman Marcus." I walked as far as Kate's car, and leaned against the hood, facing the bride and groom's shiny Mercedes.

"The one in Virginia, not the one in D.C."

"Well, hurry up, Richard. You've got to see what people are wearing to this funeral."

"All Washington women wear is black. How hard could this be?"

"Mrs. Boyd didn't get the memo. She's in red."

"I can't believe I'm missing this," Richard cried. "Don't let them start without me."

My voice caught in my throat. It couldn't be. My

mind started racing. "Of course. I can't believe I didn't think of it before."

"What? You're starting to break up, Annabelle."

My hands shook. I tried not to let the phone slip from my grasp. "I just realized something about the case, Richard."

"I'm going by the CIA. I can hardly hear you."

"They arrested the wrong person, Richard. I'm sure of it."

"This again?"

"Now I think I have the proof we need. I just need to check one thing out at home." The phone went dead. I hoped he understood me. I ran back into the church and skidded to a stop in front of Kate and Fern. They stood alone in the doorway to the sanctuary.

"That must have been some phone call," Fern said. "Your face is all flushed."

Kate brightened. "Was it Detective Reese?"

I shook my head. "I'm going to go call him, though."

"It's about time you stopped being coy," Kate said.

"I'm going to call him about the case." I lowered my voice to a whisper. "I have some new evidence for him."

"But the case is closed, Annabelle." Kate's voice almost pleaded. "Let it go."

"I can't let it go." My voice trembled with excitement. "They have the wrong person, Kate. Dr. Harriman isn't the murderer, and I know how to prove it."

Chapter 34

The organ started playing inside the sanctuary, and a few people hurried past us through the doorway.

"Go ahead inside," I said, taking Kate's car keys from her. "I have to go home and check out something, then I'm going to call Reese and give him my new evidence."

"Can't you tell us what's going on?" Kate leaned forward on the pointy toes of her high heels.

"I can't say anything out here because someone might overhear me." I gave a quick shake of my head. "You go ahead in without me. It would look odd if we all skipped the service, especially since people have already seen us."

I watched them slip into a pew close to the back, and then I tiptoed down the marble hallway and ran to Kate's car. I got in and put the key in the ignition while I called information for the District Two phone number. I splurged the extra fifty cents to be patched through directly. Driving and talking I could manage. Driving, talking, and writing down a number at the same time, I couldn't.

"I'm looking for Detective Reese," I said when a voice answered. "It's an emergency."

The cop on phone duty didn't sound impressed. "He's out. I can take a message."

"Is there any way you can reach him for me? This is

important." I steered with one hand and used my knees to hold the wheel in place. Luckily Wisconsin Avenue ran through the city in a relatively straight line.

"I can relay your message as soon as he calls in, ma'am. That's as good as I can do." I doubted that, but didn't want to get in an argument.

"Tell him Annabelle Archer called with important information about the Pierce murder case. I was at Mrs. Pierce's memorial service, but I'm heading back to my house so he can reach me on my cell phone. Please tell him it's an emergency."

"Will do."

I hung up the phone and felt like screaming. I had to talk to Reese. Where could he be? Too many thoughts were jumbled in my head. I took a deep breath to calm down. Was I right or had I jumped to conclusions?

I dialed Richard's number again and went immediately into voice mail. He must have been driving through every patch of bad reception in Washington. I left him a message telling him my hypothesis and instructing him to meet me at home, then flipped off my phone.

I passed the "social" Safeway in Upper Georgetown, where singles found shopping nights more exciting than happy hour. I turned off Wisconsin and parked a block away from my building, the tip of my car creeping into someone's brick driveway.

Could I be overreacting? Maybe my new theory was wrong and Dr. Harriman had killed his ex-wife and Mr. Boyd. No. I'd found the missing piece of the puzzle. I felt it in my gut.

Leatrice stood in the same spot we'd left her in earlier that morning. This time she had on rainbow-striped gloves. "Back so soon, dearie? Where's Kate?"

I dashed past her. "At the funeral."

"Did you forget something?" Leatrice watched me throw open the door to our building and start up the steps two at a time.

"My brain," I called out behind me. "I should have realized ages ago."

"I don't understand." Leatrice followed me inside the building and looked at me as though the head injuries had finally kicked in. "What should you have realized?"

"Never mind." I paused at the first landing. "If Detective Reese or Richard come, could you let them in, Leatrice?"

She clapped her hands. "Of course. I'll send them right up."

I ran the rest of the way up the stairs and reached my floor panting. I stumbled into my apartment and dropped the car keys on the floor. I checked the answering machine in my office while I started up my computer. No messages. That meant Reese must still be out. Didn't cops have to check in regularly?

I sat down at my computer screen and logged on to the Internet. After a few minutes of searching, I sat back and smiled. Bingo. I printed out several pages and left them in my printer while I went to the kitchen. I grabbed a Coke out of the refrigerator. Probably not the best way to calm my nerves, but I didn't care. I poured it over ice and listened to the fizz die down. I paced a few minutes before dialing the police station again.

"I'm calling for Detective Reese."

"Are you the lady who called here earlier looking for him?"

"Yes. I'm Annabelle Archer." My voice still shook.

"Okay, I gave him your message and he said he was on his way to your place."

I hung up. If I didn't know better, I'd think Reese wanted an excuse to see me. Good thing I'd been at a funeral. My black sheath dress made me look almost thin.

I fluffed the pillows on my couch and dumped my nearly empty glass of Coke in the sink. I found a can of lemon furniture polish in a bottom kitchen cabinet and walked around spraying it in the air. If it didn't look clean, at least it could smell clean. The doorbell rang and I tossed the empty can of polish in the trash.

I undid my hair from the black clip that held it back and shook it loose as I walked to the door. I pinched my cheeks and said a prayer that Richard and Kate couldn't see me. I planted a smile on my face and opened the door. My smile vanished.

It wasn't Detective Reese. It was the groom.

Chapter 35

"Dr. Donovan." My voice sounded unnaturally high-pitched. "I'm sur . . ."

"Surprised to see me?" He stepped into my apartment and pulled the door closed. "I don't know why, Miss Archer."

I tried to keep the tremor out of my voice. "Can I help you with anything?"

"For starters, you can tell me how you figured it out."

"Figured what out?" My eyes flitted to the door, which he blocked with his body.

"Don't patronize me. I overheard you tell your friends that you knew the police had arrested the wrong person." He didn't blink as he stared at me. "You didn't notice me on the other side of the sanctuary door, did you? I heard your phone ring."

I shook my head, my mouth too dry to open. I stepped back, and my legs touched the edge of the couch.

"Your phone has a distinctive ring, Miss Wedding Planner." I cursed myself for picking "Here Comes the Bride," and cursed Kate for being right when she told me it was a stupid idea. "I heard the ring when you came to pay condolences to Elizabeth, then in my office when you were snooping around, and again today. So why don't you tell me how you knew it was me."

228

I cleared my throat. "The sticker."

"What?"

"You have a window decal on your car for Andover Academy. *Phillips* Andover Academy. 'Phillips' is the only name we couldn't match up from Clara's notebook. You don't have a diploma from the prep school on your wall, though. I figured there must be a good reason for not putting it up with all the others."

"Which would be?" He sounded like a teacher coaxing a pupil.

"At first I thought you didn't go to Andover and you were willing to kill to keep that secret hidden." I took a baby step away from him. "But when I went on the school's Web site, I saw an old photo of you in the alumni section."

He crossed his hands over his chest. "Continue."

"The funny thing is that you're not listed in the alumni directory. At least Andrew Donovan isn't listed, but I suspect *you* are, aren't you?"

The groom smiled and winked at me. "Very good, Miss Archer."

I glanced at the clock on the bookshelf behind him. Where was Richard? Never mind Richard, where was Detective Reese?

"So you changed your name and that's what your mother-in-law discovered?" Mrs. Pierce's comment about changing names during the wedding started to make a lot of sense. "You killed Clara to keep your old identity a secret."

He stepped away from the door and moved toward

me. "Not bad for a wedding planner."

"You're the one who left the poisoned straw in his tuxedo jacket, not Dr. Harriman." I pointed a finger at him. Everything made sense now. "You knew Clara took medication for blood pressure and you could easily get a prescription filled."

His eye twitched. "The tuxedo jacket was a mistake."

"You ransacked my apartment trying to get it back, but you couldn't find it." I tried not to sound too victorious. "But why kill Mrs. Pierce? She adored you."

"No, she loved Andrew Donovan, Ivy League graduate. Andrew Donovan, successful doctor. Andrew Donovan, only heir of wealthy parents." His eye twitched faster. "She didn't love Andy Klump of Pittsburgh."

"You made up a fake past as well as a fake name?" I couldn't help being impressed with the extent of his lies.

"Once I got a scholarship to Andover, I promised myself I'd never be part of that blue-collar family again. I created an entirely new life for myself, complete with a family tree and ancestors going back to the Mayflower." His eye twitched in rapid fire now. "I became Andrew Donovan and couldn't even remember what it felt like to be Andy Klump."

This guy was nuts. I glanced behind me. Could I make it down the hall to the back door before he caught me? "Too bad the diploma gave you away."

"That damn Andover diploma. My future mother-in-law noticed it was missing just as you did. When she asked me about it, I told her I'd misplaced it years ago. End of story, right?" He paused and stared at me, as if waiting for me to answer.

I sidestepped the arm of the couch. "I guess not."

"She decided to surprise me by getting a copy and having it framed. Of course, when she called Andover they had no record of an Andrew Donovan. A little research into the old yearbooks turned up Andy Klump. Andy Klump who'd been dead and buried for ten years."

"So she threatened to call off the wedding and expose you." What a great story. I'd almost forgotten he wanted to kill me.

"Worse. She told me that she'd keep my secret if she had the final say in my life with Elizabeth. Where we lived, who we socialized with, which clubs we joined. Total control."

I could imagine how delighted Mrs. Pierce would have been to realize that she wouldn't be losing a daughter, she'd be gaining an indentured servant. She'd have loved blackmailing her son-in-law for the rest of her life. Part of me didn't blame him for killing her.

"I hadn't come this far and made so many sacrifices to be controlled by a society witch like Clara Pierce. I had no choice but to kill her. Don't you see?" He turned his attention to me.

I took a step backward. "Then you killed Mr. Boyd because of his relationship with Clara."

"I couldn't be sure she hadn't indulged in pillow talk,

now, could I?" He furrowed his brow, causing rows of frown lines to appear on his forehead.

"You must have switched needles when Mr. Boyd came in for his appointment with your father-in-law."

He nodded. "Easy enough to do when you share office space and have medications lying around. It's very simple to overdose on normally harmless medications, you know. Do you want to hear something funny, Miss Archer?"

Somehow I didn't think his idea of funny would be the same as mine. "Mmm-hmm."

"I had no idea about your tasting with the Boyds until the next day. Imagine my surprise when I found out that you and your caterer friend were in hot water again." He chuckled. "You must have figured it out, though, because you came sneaking around my office."

"You thought I was in your office trying to find information about you?" I kicked myself for not making the connection sooner.

"I heard your phone and guessed you must be sneaking around my office for a reason. Then when I saw you come out of the photographer's studio and Maxwell told me you'd taken my wedding pictures, I knew you were too close for comfort.

"You're the one who tried to run me off the road, aren't you?" My voice and courage were coming back. "That wasn't your Mercedes, though."

"Elizabeth's SUV. Not that she'd notice the dents with all the medication I have her on." He removed a pair of surgical latex gloves from his pants pocket. "I thought you'd be clever enough to back off."

"Why bother trying to kill me?" I swallowed hard as I saw the gloves. That explained why he didn't leave any fingerprints when he broke into my apartment. "I didn't know you were the murderer until today."

He pulled the gloves on. "You were getting too close, talking to too many people."

"Why didn't you kill Dr. Pierce, too?" I shouldn't have suggested more potential victims, but curiosity got the better of me. "Couldn't his wife have shared her secret with him, as well?"

The groom arched an eyebrow at me. "You weren't close to Clara, were you? She and her husband barely spoke. I didn't have to worry about her telling him."

He took a step toward me and my mind raced with thoughts of how to keep him talking. There was a knock on the door and I almost cheered. That would be Reese or Richard. Just in time, too.

"Yoo-hoo." Leatrice peeked inside. "It's me, dearie."

So much for my knight in shining armor.

Chapter 36

"I wasn't aware you were with someone." Leatrice gave Dr. Donovan the once-over and skipped into the room. The doctor stared at her without speaking and slipped off the gloves.

"This isn't a good time, Leatrice." I made a quick

jerky movement with my head toward the door, praying she'd take the hint and leave before Dr. Donovan decided to kill her, too.

"I'm Annabelle's neighbor, Mrs. Leatrice Butters." She took the groom's hand and pumped it.

He shot me a warning look.

"We're kind of in the middle of something, Leatrice." I darted my eyes in the groom's direction several times. Why didn't she pick up on my signals?

"Did I disturb something private?" Leatrice took a step, then pulled on Dr. Donovan's sleeve. "You should see her when she doesn't have that red bump on her forehead. She's even prettier."

Perfect. First I'd be humiliated, then I'd die.

Dr. Donovan put a hand on Leatrice's shoulder. "Mrs. Butters, we'd like a few moments alone, if you don't mind."

"Alone?" Leatrice clasped her hands together in what seemed to be the sheer joy of the moment.

"Thank you for stopping by to check on me," I said, widening my eyes and motioning my head toward the doctor. She nodded, then gave me two thumbs up before the door closed on her. What did I have to do? Send up smoke signals?

"Nice lady." Dr. Donovan leaned against the door with one hand. "It would have been too much trouble to try to kill you both at once, though."

"How do you plan to get away with all this?" My eyes darted around the room. Any heavy objects I could use to defend myself?

234

"I've gotten away with two murders so far. The police don't have a clue."

"I've already called the cops." I edged myself against the wall. "They're on their way here right now."

He took a step forward. "By the time they arrive, I'll be gone. I changed my identity once, I can do it again."

"You should escape now before they get here."

His eyes became narrow slits. "I should have killed you days ago. If you hadn't been such a busybody, I would've gotten away with it."

I wished that Reese could hear that. I narrowed my eyes. "You're not going to get away with this."

The doctor clenched and unclenched his fists. "Your bravery is only matched by your stupidity, Miss Archer."

He lunged for me, and I ran around the back of the couch. We stood on opposite sides, poised like animals ready to strike. My only chance would be to reach the back door before him. I picked up an armful of cushions and hurled it at his face, as I took off for the exit.

He swore as the cushions hit him, then I heard his feet behind me. I closed in on the doors. Just a few more feet. I felt a hand hit my back and pull me down. I screamed as my elbows hit the floor.

I twisted around onto my back, arms flailing. He raised his hands to clasp my neck as I rained punches on his face. As he tightened his grip around my throat, I heard a blood-curdling sound.

Mouth opened in a high-pitched scream, Leatrice flew through the air above us, clutching a shovel. She brought the metal down on Dr. Donovan's head, and he collapsed on top of me. Between acute hearing and shovel-wielding skills, I decided Leatrice might be a super hero in disguise. Leatrice rolled him off me with one of her brightly colored sneakers. A very good disguise.

I sat up, rubbing my throat. "How did you know, Leatrice?"

She sat down on top of him, his head between her feet. "Like I told you, I read a lot of mysteries."

"What took you so long? He almost killed me! Didn't you see the signals I sent you with my eyes?"

Leatrice reached over and patted my arm. "Yes. Next time don't be so obvious, dear. You almost gave the whole thing away."

Richard ran through the open door, gasping for breath. He saw Leatrice sitting on top of the doctor's limp body holding a shovel inches from his face and slumped against the wall. "Heard screaming . . . double parked . . . left car running . . . ran all the way . . . can't breathe . . ."

"It's over, Richard, Dr. Donovan confessed to both murders."

Richard fanned himself with both hands. "Is he dead?"

Leatrice peered through her legs at the doctor's face and raised the shovel over her head. "I don't think so. Should I hit him again?"

Chapter 37

After the police removed Dr. Donovan, barely coherent and mumbling about changing his name to Vanderbilt, I held court in my apartment. With a fresh new lump on my head, I figured I should be calling the shots. Leatrice and Kate sat on either side of me on the couch, taking turns holding the ice pack on my head. Richard had risen to the occasion, preparing an impressive display of cold hors d'oeuvres, considering the contents of my kitchen.

Detective Reese perched on the edge of my overstuffed chair, taking small bites of a tomato and Velveeta canapé that Fern insisted he try. He wore a black knit shirt that stretched over the muscles in his arms. I concentrated hard on not noticing.

"Can you believe that Richard didn't want to use this perfectly good cheese? Those expiration dates are just guidelines." Fern pointed a thumb toward Richard in the kitchen. Reese stopped in midbite and placed the hors d'oeuvre on a lavender monogrammed cocktail napkin. Fern gave a loud sniff and retreated to the kitchen.

Kate tucked her legs under her. "I can't believe Dr. Donovan was the murderer."

"He covered well, setting up his father-in-law." Reese picked up his notepad from the table. He'd almost filled it when he arrived and questioned us.

Now he was on the last page. "We would have discovered him eventually, though."

I lifted the ice pack off my head. "You mean after he'd killed me, changed his identity, and moved to another country?"

"Don't excite yourself, dearie." Leatrice pushed the ice back on lump number two.

"He'd have stayed put if you hadn't gone around stirring up trouble, Annabelle." Reese folded his arms across his broad chest.

I forced myself to look a few inches north and meet his eyes, which seemed to turn greener as we argued. "You're saying it's my fault he tried to kill me . . . twice?"

Leatrice gave a nervous laugh. "I'm sure that's not what Detect . . ."

"If you hadn't stuck your nose in the investigation, he wouldn't have felt threatened enough to kill you," Reese insisted.

"I can't believe this." I sat up quickly, felt a pain in my head, and leaned back. "We solve this case and present the killer to you on a silver platter, and you still won't give us any credit."

He nodded his head at Leatrice. "I'll give credit for the most creatively subdued suspect."

I thought of the groom being carried out with clumps of mulch from Leatrice's shovel clinging to his face and tried not to smile. I wanted to focus on outrage!

Leatrice turned bright pink. "I just worked with what I had."

Richard came out of the kitchen followed by Fern, who carried what appeared to be a plate of pinwheels made out of luncheon meat and something gooey. He gave a weak sigh as I eyed the plate Fern set on the coffee table. "This day has been one disaster after another."

"There, there." Fern put an arm around Richard. "Don't you worry about a thing. Try one of my yogurt pinwheels."

Richard peeked through his fingers at the drippy hors d'oeuvre Fern held up. "Heaven preserve me."

Kate raised an eyebrow at Richard, then leaned over toward Reese. "I can't believe the groom killed his own mother-in-law. We didn't have a clue before today."

I noticed her blouse hanging open, and pulled her back next to me. "Actually we had plenty of clues. The victims being killed with prescription drugs, the tuxedo with the powder residue . . ."

"I guess you're right," Kate jumped in. "Don't forget 'Phillips' written in Mrs. Pierce's notebook and the missing diploma."

"We didn't even make the connection that Dr. Donovan worked in the same office as his father-in-law," I added. "It never occurred to us that the killer could be someone so charming."

"Or so handsome." Kate grinned at Reese. I pinched her hard on the leg. She yelped, glaring at me, and I noticed Reese trying to contain a smile. I reminded myself that cocky policemen weren't my type. Reese caught my eye and gave me a small wink. I smiled at him in spite of my best efforts not to and felt my face get warm. Then, again, a little adventure in life wasn't bad.

"Sometimes it's who you least expect." Leatrice cleared her throat. "Appearances can be deceiving."

Kate shrugged her shoulders. "I guess all that glitters isn't mold."

Center Point Publishing
600 Brooks Road • PO Box 1
Thorndike ME 04986-0001 USA

(207) 568-3717

US & Canada:
1 800 929-9108